D1480896

let
sleeping
dogs
lie

let sleeping dogs lie

A MYSTERY BY
JOHN R. RIGGS

DEMBNER BOOKS · NEW YORK

Dembner Books
Published by Red Dembner Enterprises Corp.,
80 Eighth Avenue, New York, N.Y. 10011
Distributed by W. W. Norton & Company, Inc.,
500 Fifth Avenue, New York, N.Y. 10110

Library of Congress Cataloging in Publication Data

Riggs, John R., 1945–
   Let sleeping dogs lie.

   I. Title.
PS3568.I372L48 1986   813'.54   85-25275
ISBN 0-934878-67-6

To Mike Bailey,
the best of friends

let
sleeping
dogs
lie

1

I picked up the receiver and put it down again. Picked it up and put it down. Started to pick it up one more time. . . .

"For God's sake," Ruth said, "call her. If you don't, I will!"

"No."

"Why not?"

"Because she's the one who moved away. I didn't."

"Who are you trying to punish, her or yourself or me? Because if you're underfoot one more Saturday, I'm going to start tearing my hair out by the handfuls!"

Ruth is a tall, big-boned Swede with grey-blond hair, a withering scowl, and all the finesse of a steamroller. She's somewhere between sixty and seventy—she won't say where—and has been my housekeeper for five and a half years now, ever since I moved to Oakalla following the death of my grandmother Ryland. That is exactly five and a half years longer than either of us expected her to stay.

How we've survived—especially that first week when she was looking for a shovel to hit me with, while I was looking for an ax to return the favor—I don't know. Maybe it's because we don't dwell on our differences (and there are plenty of those). Maybe it's because she's a gambler at heart. So am I. We'll bet on anything—from a hog-calling contest to the color of Lassie's right front paw. And maybe it's because we both like to fly by the seat of our pants without too much worry where we'll land. As Ruth is fond of saying, she'd rather burn out than rust out. Amen.

The "she" we were arguing about is Diana Baldwin, who left Oakalla a little over a month ago to return to school at the University of Wisconsin in Madison. It seems more like a year. I'm Garth Ryland, editor of the *Oakalla Reporter*, the weekly newspaper in town. Usually on Saturday I'm out and about. But not this Saturday.

"I'm not trying to punish anyone," I said. "Diana said she'd call. She hasn't. There must be a reason."

"Which is?"

"I don't know."

"Then why don't you call her and find out?"

"Because it's her decision. Not mine."

Ruth's face brightened. "Now we're getting to the heart of the matter. You *are* trying to punish her. Make her pay for what she's doing."

"No, I'm not."

"Then what are you trying to do?"

"Give her what she wants. She said she wanted to be free, to see life on her own for a while. Then she'd make her decision about us. I've already made my decision. So the only thing for me to do is give her all the space she wants."

"And in the meantime you're not going to go out of your way to make things easy for her?"

"Why should I? I want her here with me in Oakalla.

10

It's not in my best interest to make it easier for her to stay away."

"What about her best interest?"

"She knows my number. If she really needs me, she can call."

"And you'll come running?"

"I don't know what I'll do."

She sighed. "That makes two of us. Another month of this and I'll be ready for Woodhollow Sanitarium. You say it's her life, that win or lose she has to get on with it and see for herself what she wants. Then why don't you get on with yours and quit moping around here, waiting for the phone to ring, making us both miserable."

"Because there's nothing I want to do today."

"You never had any trouble before."

"That's because Saturday was Diana's and my day. We always spent part of it together, even when Fran was alive."

"That was your first mistake, taking up with a married woman."

"You know we didn't take up. We just fell into it."

"Well, now you've fallen out of it. So find something else to occupy your time and give me a little space while you're at it."

The phone rang. I thought I heard Ruth praying in the background. "Garth, this is Bill Airhart. Did you forget about me?"

"Why?"

"You were supposed to pick me up a half hour ago. With that car of yours, I thought maybe you were hung up somewhere."

"That's right. I forgot." Today was the day of our yearly grouse hunt. "I'll be there in fifteen minutes."

"I'll be waiting on the porch."

"Diana?" Ruth asked hopefully when I hung up.

"Doc Airhart. We're going grouse hunting."

She smiled her broadest smile in years. "Any port in a storm."

I went upstairs, changed clothes, and took my single-shot sixteen gauge Stevens from the closet. I'd bought the Stevens with my paper-route money when I was thirteen. It was the first shotgun I ever owned, and the first time I shot it, it put me into the cheap seats. One shot still left my shoulder black and blue. But of all the shotguns I'd ever owned—and I'd owned several over the years—it was still first in my heart.

I got in Jezebel, alias Jessie, my grandmother Ryland's brown Chevy sedan, and backed out of the garage. So far so good. Any time I got her this far it was a major victory for both of us.

I inherited Jessie along with Grandmother Ryland's small farm. I'm not sure why I've kept Jessie all this time. God knows I've had enough reasons to tie her to the nearest railroad track. But she was faithful in her own way (she wouldn't run for anyone else either) and she had the character I found lacking in today's cars. She wasn't a Caprice or an Impala or an Antelope or an Orangutan. She was first, last, and always—a Chevy.

Doc Airhart sat on his porch waiting for me. He was a gnarled bony wisp of a man whose fine white hair hung in tufts from beneath his red hunting cap. He wore brown hunting pants, a red wool shirt patched at the elbows, a down hunting vest, and held his trusty Browning, an over-and-under twenty gauge with one barrel a modified choke and the other an improved cylinder. His old setter, Belle, sat beside him, wearing the same look of patience as Doc. They'd both been around too long to get in a hurry.

Doc climbed in the front seat beside me. I held the door open while Belle climbed in the back. Outside of Topsy, Grandmother Ryland's collie, she was the only dog to ever ride in Jessie. On warm days she sat with her head out the window, taking in the breeze as we rode along. On cold days she curled up on the back seat, sighed occasionally, and dreamed deep setter dreams.

"I see you made it," Doc said.

"Finally. Thanks for calling to remind me." I put Jessie in gear. "Where to?" I asked.

"A special place. I'll bet you've never been there before. Have to tell you how to get there."

"There any grouse there?"

"There used to be. Lots of them."

"How long ago?"

He thought a moment. It seemed a cloud crossed his face as he did. "Almost forty years now."

"You sure it's still there? A lot can change in forty years."

"It's still there. Was the last time I looked anyway."

"When was that?"

"One day last week." His face said he didn't want to discuss it further. So I didn't.

I drove while Doc gave directions. We went north to the end of Fair Haven Road, turned east, went about a mile, then turned back south again. The road began to wind and narrow, as it led deeper into a thick stand of spruce. Toward its end it became two leaf-strewn ruts that stopped at a huge stone pillar. Before us were the remains of what had once been a farm, its rolling fields now trees, shrubs, and brambles, and a perfect place to hunt grouse. Considering some of the other places he'd taken me, I wondered why Doc had never brought me here before.

We got out and stretched while Belle sniffed the nearest bush and made her customary pit stop. It was a beautiful October morning without a cloud or a wind to spoil it. Just a smoky-blue sky and the sun laying down its warmth in gentle golden swaths. I took a deep breath and smiled. Ruth was right. I did feel better out here.

Belle led the way, as Doc and I followed about twenty yards apart. Belle was a slow worker, so it wasn't hard to keep up. That's the way I liked it. It gave me time to kick every bush to see what was under it.

Not that it mattered. In the five years we'd hunted together, neither Doc nor I had bagged any grouse. Either

Doc was a consummately bad shot, or he just wasn't trying, and I never bothered to put a shell in my gun. The only things we had bagged so far were a pheasant that flew into a fence and broke his neck and a deer hunter who bailed out of his tree stand when Doc absent-mindedly pointed his Browning at him while scratching a chigger bite.

So what was the point in going hunting in the first place? It gave me a chance to enjoy the company of a grand old man. Dr. William T. Airhart, "Doc" as we all called him, had practiced medicine for fifty years until he'd retired at age seventy-five, five years ago. I'd been his patient as a boy. He'd been to see me at Grandmother's farm. I remember he had a square needle and the voice of Billy Goat Gruff, but somehow I felt better the minute he walked into my room. I still feel better around him. His mischievous smile and twinkling blue eyes seem to say, "Come on, Garth, don't take it all so seriously." I occasionally need to be reminded of that. Especially now that I'd turned forty and Diana had left town.

We walked a ridge, followed it into a ravine and along a creek bottom, climbed another ridge through a thick stand of scrub oak, and came out in what was once a pasture. Belle had gone on point twice so far and had a bird each time—one grouse and one woodcock, both of which Doc had missed. He grumbled to me about it, but it seemed that after each miss, he and Belle looked at each other and smiled.

"Getting hungry?" Doc asked.

"I'm past that," I answered.

"We'll stop in a minute. I know just the place."

I followed him through the pasture, across a broken-down gate, and into a clearing. A ramshackle barn stood in the center of the clearing. Beside the barn a spring flowed from a clay tile, and its cold sweet water was about the best I'd ever tasted. I knelt beside it and drank my fill, then took a look around.

The spring fed a small rocky creek, which bounced

14

merrily along, gurgling and bubbling and making peaceful creek music. To the west was a stone chimney where perhaps a log house and stone fireplace had once sat and beyond that three rows of Norway pines, planted as windbreak. It looked like a fire had destroyed the house and blackened the chimney, probably long ago.

"What do you think?" Doc asked.

"You were right. You knew just the place." I looked from the barn to the sky. The setting was peace itself. "Do you have any idea who owns it?" I asked.

"I own it."

"Since when?"

Again a shadow crossed his face. "Since Armageddon" was all he'd say.

We walked up to the ruins of the house and sat in the shade of the pines. Doc pulled three chicken salad sandwiches from his hunting vest—one for him, one for Belle, and one for me—along with some dill pickles and oranges. I'd been after his recipe for the chicken salad for the past five years, but he refused, saying he kept it in his head and was afraid to write it down for fear he might have to follow it. I knew what he meant, so I didn't push it.

It soon grew cool in the shade, so we moved back out into the sunlight where I stretched out on the ground. With the sun on my face and the smell of sun-baked pine in the air, I felt more at ease than I had since the night Diana left. If the wind didn't shift and the sun didn't set, I might have stayed there forever. When I glanced at Doc, I could see he felt the same way.

"Were you ever poor?" I asked.

He opened his eyes momentarily, then closed them again. "For a long time I was without money. But I can't say I've ever been poor."

"Good point."

"Why do you ask?"

"A thought that's been bothering me for a long time. I've never had much money. I've always had enough to get by but never any extra to spend on myself or someone else I thought was worth it. And the one time I did, after Grandmother died and left me some, I bought the *Reporter* and was right back in the same boat. I just wonder what it would have been like to be suddenly rich, if that would have changed me in any way?"

"For the better or worse?" Doc asked.

"Either one. Has it changed you?"

Again his eyes fluttered open and closed again. "That's hard to say. I was without money for so long it was hard to get used to it once I had it. For years I still bought the cheapest I could get by with because that's what I'd always done. Not for my medical practice, there I always demanded the best. But for me personally. Then one day I decided that since I could afford the best, why not buy the best? So that's what I did. And I'm not sorry. I think my life's richer because of it. Not just for the things I own and the places I've been. They're not worth much by them- selves—they can't put in what your soul leaves out—but because they're the frosting on the cake. I could get by without them all right, but life wouldn't be quite as sweet."

"But you yourself haven't changed?"

"Of course I have. We all do with time. But not so I don't recognize myself."

"That's what I was asking."

Doc opened his eyes and sat up. His gaze went to the barn and the surrounding woods. He was seeing some- thing in the past, something he'd rather not have seen. "But I will say this. Too much money *can* corrupt you. Too much of anything can, whether it's money, power, fame, or what have you. The sheer weight of it is too much for most of us to bear."

I sat up beside him. "How much is too much?"

"How high is the sky? We all have our limits. The stronger we are, the farther they take us before we break. But we've all been broken by temptation. Either that or we lose touch and start thinking we have the right to do

16

whatever it is we want to do just because we want it. The very rich seem to have that problem. So do the very powerful."

"Aren't they one and the same?"

"Usually, but not always."

"What about the very beautiful?"

"Them too. They seem to fall the hardest. Perhaps because they least expect it."

I glanced around the area. If any place was the perfect setting for a farm, this was the place. Still it was abandoned. It made me wonder. "Maybe that's what happened here," I said.

"What's that?"

"Take a look around. Whoever was here last didn't stay. Maybe it was just too beautiful, too easy to sit and think and watch the sunset, instead of plowing the lower forty."

Doc looked away. "Maybe it was at that."

"It's not your homeplace, is it?"

"No, not mine."

"Whose then? Do you know?"

He gave me a strange look. On anyone else it would have been frightening. "Beelzebub's."

"You wouldn't mind explaining that, would you?"

"Yes, Garth, I'm afraid I would."

We hunted the rest of the afternoon. Belle pointed three more grouse. Three more times Doc shot and missed. One bird flew my way and I had it covered all the way to the tamaracks. When I lowered the Stevens without firing, Doc just shook his head and walked on. By now he was on to me, as I was to him.

Toward evening we stopped on the knoll by the stone chimney. Doc picked the burs out of Belle's coat, and I went down to the barn for one last drink before heading home. While I was there, I decided to have a look inside the barn. I was a scrounge at heart and who knew what treasures might be inside? According to Doc, this place hadn't had much traffic for the past forty years.

The big sliding door on the front of the barn was wedged shut from the inside, but I found a loose board and crawled through. As I did something scampered for hiding, and a large thick bird, likely an owl, flew out through a broken window above me. It took a moment for my eyes to adjust to the dark, and when they did, I saw a large mound of straw piled on the floor of the barn.

I moved closer. The straw was brown and rotten and smelled like the inside of a tennis shoe. It also had a car's bumper sticking out of it. I felt my heart go thumpety-thump. A bumper might mean there was a car attached.

I dug into the straw to find out. The farther I went, the faster my heart began to beat. The car was a convert-ible. And it was a Cadillac. The trademark told me so. But I didn't know what year. When I could find my voice, I called Doc in for his opinion.

He knew at a glance. "It's a 1936 Cadillac convertible sedan," he said.

"Do you know who it belongs to?"

"No, I don't."

Then he turned and abruptly left, nearly stepping on Belle as he did. Strange. I thought he'd be as thrilled as I was. He wasn't. In fact, he was almost hostile. No matter, I'd think about it later.

I walked around the Cadillac, smiling to myself, not able to believe my good fortune. This was a dream come true. Not mine. Ruth's. She always talked with a special glow about a 1936 Cadillac convertible, that if there was one thing she could own before she died that would be it. Not just any 1936 Cadillac convertible. She had a particu-lar one in mind, I was sure. And the more I thought about it, the unlikelihood that there were two 1936 Cadillac convertibles floating around a town the size of Oakalla, the more certain I was that this was the one she always talked

18

about. Even better, her birthday was only three weeks away.

That meant something had to be wrong with it. I never was that lucky. I put my smile away and took a closer look. The finish was gone. Moisture had leached through the straw and ruined it. There was rust on the chrome that needed sanding and also some rust around both of the sidemounts. And the top, which was up, had rotted in a couple of places and would need to be patched until it could be replaced.

But all in all the Cadillac was in good shape. The tires, though flat, looked to be sound. The body was well preserved, and except for an inch of dust covering everything the interior looked as good as new. I raised the hood just to make sure. Yes. There was an engine under it.

Finally I found something to worry about. The Cadillac wasn't mine. It was also worth more than I could ever pay for it. I remembered hearing that a 1929 Dusenberg had recently been appraised at five hundred thousand dollars. Though the Cadillac probably wasn't in that class, I was sure it was worth more than the dollar ninety-eight, plus tax, that I could afford. That meant I had two alternatives. I could seek out its owner and try to buy it for a song, or I could steal it outright. I never could sing.

Doc was already sitting in Jessie when I got there. He didn't speak to me all the way back to Oakalla, and when I thanked him for the hunt, he just grunted and slammed the door. Even Belle seemed to have caught his mood. Usually she snored contentedly on the way home. Today she whined and thrashed. And when he opened the door for her to get out, she moaned at the effort. Together they limped up the steps and into the house.

2

The next morning while Ruth was outside raking the yard, I made a call to Pete Hammond. Tall and gangling with hollow cheeks and a thimble for a nose, Pete was a jack-of-all-trades and one of the few people Oakalla couldn't do without for long. He was also wired to about two thousand volts and a chain smoker. Just being on the same block with him made me nervous. But if you needed something done in a hurry, you called on Pete. I needed something done in a hurry.

"I'm free right now," Pete said.

"Give me five minutes. I want to make another phone call."

"I'll give you ten. That way I can fill up with gas."

I called Doc Airhart. He answered on the third ring. "Doc, this is Garth. How would you like to take a ride with Pete Hammond and me?"

"That depends. Where are you going?"

"Out to pick up that Cadillac I found yesterday."

"Sorry, I'm not interested." The tone of his voice made that plain.

"But I do have your permission to go onto your land after it?"

"You don't have my permission. But if you're set on going, I suppose I can't stop you."

"I'm set on going."

"Then that's that." He hung up.

That wasn't like Doc. We all had our moods, but his were never very black or very long. That was one of the reasons I liked being around him. He seemed to have made his peace with life. For those of us still struggling, it was good to see it could be done.

I met Pete uptown a few minutes later. We retraced the route Doc and I had traveled yesterday. Pete drove with his left hand, and his right bounced from the steering wheel to his mouth, as he took one drag after another on his cigarette. He drove about as fast as he smoked. I gritted my teeth and held on.

Pete snuffed his cigarette against the dash and threw it out the window. Within seconds he lit another one. "This is legal, isn't it, what we're doing?" he asked.

"Ask me no questions, I'll tell you no lies."

"This truck is my bread and butter. I don't want them to impound it."

"Where we're going, Pete, the only thing likely to impound it is the deer."

"You're sure about that?"

"You'll see when we get there."

He saw when we got there. "There's no road here."

"You're right, Pete."

"How do we get to the barn?"

"We make our own."

"We'll never make it."

"Sure we will. Just follow me."

I got out of the flatbed and started walking toward the

barn, trying to stay on the high ground and along the lane that used to be here. Pete followed a short distance behind and kept racing the motor just to see if I was awake. By the time we reached the ruins of the house, I wasn't sure which of us needed a cigarette more.

Then, down to his last ounce of patience, he cut around me and started for the barn. He missed driving into an open well by about the width of a tire. The well had filled in over the years until the dirt was about three feet from the top. Still it would have been hard for Pete and me to lift the flatbed out by hand.

"What was that I just missed up there?" Pete asked when I got to the barn.

"A well."

"Holy Christ! You didn't tell me that was there!"

"Now you know."

He looked at me like I was crazy. He was probably right.

After sliding open the barn door and clearing away the timbers from around the Cadillac, we put down the skids, winched it up onto the flatbed, chocked it in place, and covered it with a tarpaulin that I'd found in the basement. An hour later we were back in Oakalla.

We stopped in front of Edgar Shoemaker's welding shop. Edgar had only one lung and sight in one eye, but he was the best body man in Adams County. He also had a lot of grit. He'd lost the lung in World War II, the eye to a piece of hot steel, but that hadn't slowed him down any. If anything, it made him even more determined. And contrary. He worked his own hours whether you liked it or not.

I went inside the shop where the smoke was so thick I couldn't see Edgar at first, only the sparks from his welder. After feeling my way through the maze of junk on the floor, I saw he was welding the frame for a car. When he finally saw me, he turned off the welder, flipped up his mask, and picked up his cigar that was lying on top of the

22

frame. He sucked on it a couple of times, then gave it up for dead.

"What's on your mind, Garth?" he asked. "I got started today on something that should've been done yesterday."

"I've got something I want to show you."

"How long will it take?"

"Not long. It's just outside."

He followed me out, climbed up on the flatbed, and looked under the tarp. Then he carefully put the tarp back down and whistled softly to himself. "Where'd you find it?" he asked.

"Grouse hunting," I answered.

He nodded. He knew me well enough not to ask anything more about its origin. "What do you plan to do with it?"

"I thought I'd turn it over to you."

He shook his head. "I can't, Garth. I'm covered up right now. I don't know when I'll be uncovered."

"I can wait."

"How long?"

"Three weeks."

He shook his head again. "I wouldn't even get started. Something like that, you just can't hurry. It's like an iceberg. For every spot of rust you can see, there's a lot more beneath the surface."

I was disappointed. I had been sure Edgar would be able to restore the Cadillac. I didn't know anyone else I'd trust with it.

"Why don't you try Woody?" he suggested. "He probably has the time."

I didn't doubt that. Time was about the only thing Woody did have. Woody Padgett, Edgar's first cousin, lived on Paul Black's farm and worked on and off as Paul's hired hand, whenever Paul needed him. Woody stayed by himself in a one room house that only a pigeon could love, wore bib overalls everywhere he went, and had a perpetual look of astonishment on his face, as if even the sunrise were a puzzle to him.

His given name wasn't Woody. It was Elmer or Elmo or something like that. Ruth knew what it was, but then there wasn't much about Oakalla she didn't know. Woody was a nickname given in childhood. Ruth said it was because he was as dense as a blue beech. Others said it was because he spent a lot more time in the woods than he ever did in school.

I didn't know, really didn't care. Even if he wasn't the last of the late great thinkers, Woody had a good heart and perhaps the wisest hands I'd ever seen. There was nothing he couldn't do with a piece of wood, whether making willow whistles for the kids in town or carving a block of oak into a centerpiece. And his decoys, once carved and painted, would sit right up and quack at you. But I didn't know he did body work.

"He doesn't very often," Edgar said. "But he can. Taught me everything I know, if you can believe that. Most don't."

"Then he's good?" I wanted to make sure. I'd wait until Edgar was free if there was any doubt.

"He's the best there is," Edgar answered, then went back inside his shop.

"Well?" Pete asked when I climbed inside the flatbed.

"Edgar said to take it to Woody."

"You going to?"

"Would you?"

"Where else you going to take it?"

Sometimes Pete was a master of logic.

I found Woody in the barn he used as a workshop. He was knee deep in tractor parts and looked like he'd spent the night in an oil barrel. "Can you spare a couple minutes?" I asked.

Woody frowned at me. He looked more perplexed than usual, like he'd lost something. It was the first time I'd ever seen him in a hurry. Then he handed me a socket wrench. "Here, you turn and I'll hold. Paul wants this thing back together by tonight."

I tightened the nut while he held the bolt. "What's his hurry?" I asked.

"He's got a field of beans he needs to combine. He's afraid they'll get down before he gets them out."

"Not much chance of that is there?" I asked, knowing that Woody liked to talk weather as much as I did.

He looked out at the dark blue sky, then smiled at me. "No. Not much chance of that."

I handed him back his wrench and he put on another socket. I tried it on the nut. It was too small. "I think I need a three-quarter," I said.

Woody sorted through his sockets, but he wasn't looking very hard for the one I needed. He kept glancing up at the flatbed, as Pete stood in front of it smoking his third cigarette since we'd arrived. "Pete seems to have the willies," Woody observed.

"I think he's running late," I said.

Woody laid his wrench down and stood up. "Pete's always running late. But I guess I can spare a couple of minutes."

I nodded to Pete and he jumped onto the flatbed and undid the tarp. At first Woody just gazed at the Cadillac with his mouth open, like a kid at his first burlesque show. Then a smile spread from ear to ear, as he climbed onto the flatbed and gingerly touched the fender of the Cadillac, as if touching the face of an old friend recently returned from the dead.

"Where'd you find this?" he asked.

I gave him my stock answer. "Grouse hunting."

"Where?" he persisted.

"Around."

"North or south of town?"

"Northeast." Pete answered for me. He was ready to unload the Cadillac and get out of here. I was ready to stuff the tarpaulin in his mouth. The less said about the Cadillac the better.

"How far?"

"Far enough." I beat Pete to the punch. "What I want to know is are you interested in restoring it or not?"

Woody didn't answer. He continued to gaze at the Cadillac, like it was his lost child. "It's a thirty-six, isn't it?"

"Yes, it is," I answered, wondering how he knew.

Meanwhile Pete lit another cigarette and turned his back on both of us. He could hear his phone ringing at home. The fifty dollars he was charging me already seemed like a bad bargain. Little did either of us realize how bad a bargain it was.

"I thought so," Woody said.

"Do you think you can restore it?" I repeated.

He seemed to understand for the first time what I was asking. "Sure. I'd love to."

"How long do you think it'll take?"

"Not long. Not long at all." There was a dreamlike tone to his voice. If I hadn't known him better, I'd have sworn he was on something.

"Could you have it done in three weeks?"

"Easy."

"What about Paul Black's tractor?"

"What about it?"

"Don't you have to finish it first?"

"Sure. I'll have it done tonight."

With Superman's help, maybe, but I didn't argue. "You're sure you can finish it in three weeks? It's important."

"What's that?" Woody had moved forward to look inside the Cadillac. He was back in his own world again.

"Never mind. Why don't I leave the Cadillac here. You can look it over and then call me tomorrow to tell me what it'll cost and how long it's going to take."

"Sure. Anything you say."

I nodded to Pete and he began to put down the skids.

"What are you doing?" Woody asked sharply.

"Unloading the Cadillac," I said.

"Not here. In the barn."

"There's a tractor in the way."

"I'll make room."

He was as good as his word. In ten minutes we had more than enough room. And throughout the unloading, until the Cadillac was safely inside the barn, Woody's eyes never left it, never allowed us one moment of carelessness. And by the time we were outside, I was certain he'd forgotten all about the tractor and Paul Black's beans. I was also certain he knew more about the Cadillac than I did.

3

Monday came and went slowly, as most of my Mondays usually do. I'd been inside all day wanting out, but couldn't get more than an arm's length away from the phone. "Yes, Mrs. Collins, I did know that Poopsie had puppies last week. You called to tell me. No, Mrs. Collins, I don't think eight is a world's record, not even for a miniature poodle. Yes, I'll be sure to look it up. Thank you so much for calling."

And so it went in typical Monday fashion. But today I didn't seem to mind as much, and my patience was longer than usual. I kept thinking about the Cadillac and how pleased Ruth would be to have it. She deserved it. After putting up with me for five and a half years, that was the least I could do for her.

At home later that day I found Ruth holding a bug bomb in one hand and a fly swatter in the other. She was tracking down the cricket that so far had made a shambles of her day. Together we moved the stove, the refrigerator, the dinette, and the kitchen cabinet, but still no cricket. "Cheep! Cheep! Cheep!" He sounded like he had a megaphone. I looked at Ruth whose hand tightened on the bug bomb. I knew with the next cheep every living thing within a hundred square feet was going to be annihilated. I took the bug bomb away from her. I wasn't going to wait for the lightning to hit.

"What are you doing?" she demanded.

"Enough is enough."

"What do you mean, enough is enough? We haven't found him yet."

"He'll keep until tomorrow."

"That coming from the man who for four straight hours threw his pillow at the ceiling trying to kill a mosquito! You've sure turned mellow in your old age."

"It was for three hours and he'd kept me up all week."

"What about the neighbor's dog, the time you threw the cherry bomb on top of his doghouse?"

"He deserved it. You and I both agreed. You should talk. You were going to turn the hose on him."

"I would have, too, if I'd got the nozzle to work."

I sat at the kitchen table, putting the bug bomb under my chair where she couldn't get at it. "So, except for the cricket, how did your day go?"

"About the same as usual. Monday never changes much."

I saw the mums I'd sent her sitting on the sink. "Nothing at all out of the ordinary?"

"Diana didn't call, if that's what you're asking."

"What about Woody Padgett?"

"Him either."

That bothered me.

She washed her hands and dried them on the dish towel. "What do you and Woody have cooking?"

"Not much. He's doing a little work for me."

"What kind of work?"

"This and that. It doesn't amount to much. I thought I might have him carve you a decoy for your birthday."

"What would I do with a decoy?" She was rummaging through the bottom of the stove, looking for the right pan.

"Who knows when one might come in handy."

She found the pan she was looking for and put it on the stove. "You're right. You never know when you might run out of firewood. Speaking of which, we're about out."

"I've got a load coming in tomorrow."

"It's about time. What made you think of it?"

"I just felt like a fire, that's all."

"First time this year."

"Right. First time this year." My first since Diana had left.

"You going to build one tonight?"

"Maybe later. I'll have to see how tonight goes. Tomorrow for sure."

"I plan to hold you to it."

"See that you do."

"You have to rejoin the living sometime."

"I know that. But knowing and doing are two different things. Though today I feel better. The best I have in a long time. I only lost one subscriber."

"Not bad for a Monday."

"No, not bad at all."

"Is that why you sent me the flowers?"

"How did you know they were from me?"

"Who else would send me flowers?"

"Dane Stewart used to."

"Dane Stewart used to send flowers to the Knights of Columbus and the Odd Fellows Hall and about twenty-six other places I know of. He even sent some to the White House once."

"What's wrong with that?"

"He sent them by Pony Express."

"Okay. I get your point. But do you like them?"

"What?" She was busy cutting up an onion.

30

"The flowers."

"Why wouldn't I?"

"No reason, I guess."

"You'd like me to jump up and down, is that it?"

"Diana always did. Well, close anyway."

"Then why didn't you send them to her?"

"Because I wanted to send them to you."

"And I appreciate them. It's not often I get flowers from a man. The closest thing Karl ever came to it was a rubber plant one Easter. And it died before fall. Scraggly little thing, I don't know why he bothered." Her eyes were watery. I couldn't tell if it was from the onions or her memories of Karl.

In a way I envied her. I sometimes wondered if I'd ever have those lifetime memories of someone, if any in my generation would. At forty, one marriage and at least half a lifetime were already behind me. And except for my family, who was miles away, there was nobody who knew me now that knew me when.

"Well, I'm glad you like them," I said.

"Glad enough to get out of my kitchen? I like your company, but I can't talk and cook at the same time."

I left, taking the bug bomb with me. Otherwise, the temptation might prove too much for her. When she called me back for supper, I noticed she had moved the flowers to the center of the kitchen table.

After supper I got in Jessie and went out to see Woody. I still hadn't heard from him, and while I didn't think he'd steal the Cadillac, he seemed to have an extraordinary interest in it. That meant he might know its owner. And the last thing I wanted was for the owner, whoever it might be, to find out about the Cadillac. The Cadillac hadn't walked to where it was. Somebody had to have driven it. Why would someone drive it way out there and hide it under a straw stack? I could think of only one reason. It had probably been stolen.

Woody lived southwest, about two miles from town,

along what we called the Crick Road. Or the Creek Road, if you were a purist. The first mile of the road was asphalt; the rest of it was gravel. A cloud of dust about thirty feet wide followed me all the way to Woody's drive.

No lights were on in the house. I climbed out of Jessie and knocked on the door. No one answered. I knocked again, then looked inside. No sign of Woody anywhere. No sign of his battered red Ford pickup either.

I went to the barn and stoped at the sliding door. By now it was nearly dark outside and darker inside. I called, but no one answered. Odd, I thought, since the door was partially open.

I hesitated before going inside. I'd been in dark barns before, sparrow hunting as a boy, and they weren't my favorite places to be. Too many things lived in there, cats and chickens included. I never knew when one would come sailing out at me.

I took a step inside and let my eyes adjust. Somewhere around was a light switch, if I could only find it. I spent the next five minutes looking for it, bumping into things as I went. When I did find it and turned it on, I could have saved myself the trouble. Woody wasn't in here either. But Paul Black's tractor was—just as we'd left it yesterday. So was the Cadillac.

I went outside and called for him, but again no one answered. I decided to wait for a while on the chance that he'd gone into town for something. I went back inside the barn, pulled a bale of hay down from the mow, and sat on the floor of the barn with my back resting against the bale. It was cool but not uncomfortable there, and I began to drowse. Then I heard the leaves rustle in the woods just beyond the barn. I awakened with a start. "Woody?" I called.

No answer. Probably an animal.

I walked to the back door of the barn and took a long look at the woods outside. It seemed to have moved two feet closer to the barn since the last time I looked.

I closed the barn door and walked to the front door to close it when I heard a car start up. I looked up and down Creek Road but saw nothing.

I wondered where the car could be. Then I remembered the dead end road that led south off Creek Road about two hundred yards west of where I was standing. I couldn't see the dead end road for the trees, but I thought I heard gravel crunching under someone's tires.

I went outside for a better look, caught a glimpse of the moon reflecting off chrome. I was hoping the car would come my way, but it went the other way instead. Finally, about a half mile down the road, it turned on its lights. I could see them spraying the tops of the trees as it went west, then south.

I debated on what to do next. If I went home now, chances were that Woody would arrive within the next five minutes. If I stayed and waited on him, no telling when he would be here. I didn't want to leave the Cadillac here alone. Nor did I particularly want to stay and miss a night's sleep—another night's sleep, one of many lately.

Hoping he'd forgive me, I went back into Woody's house and turned on all the lights I could find. I returned to the barn and did the same. When I was sure I had enough light to fool someone into thinking a lot of us were there, I slipped out the back door of the barn and walked home. I left Jessie to guard the place in my absence.

4

Early the next morning Ruth was waiting for me in the kitchen. She had my juice and cereal poured—surprisingly not in the same bowl—my coffee perking, and a cinnamon coffee cake cooling on top of the oven. She was killing me with kindness. She sometimes tried that when all else failed.

I cut myself a piece of coffee cake and ate it while waiting for the coffee to finish perking. "Where did you go last night?" she asked. "I waited up until ten."

"Out to Woody Padgett's."

"What were you doing out there?"

"Waiting for Woody."

"I see. That's okay. You don't have to tell me."

"Tell you what?"

"What you were doing out there."

"I told you last night. He's making something for me. But he didn't show up."

"Is that why you walked home?"

"How do you know I walked?"

"I heard you come in."

"I thought you were in bed."

"I was. But I know when a car pulls up out back, especially yours. I heard you come in the door, but I didn't hear that rattletrap of yours coming down the alley like I usually do."

Ruth had a fondness for Jessie, matched only by her love of pythons and cobras. "Okay, I walked home. Is there anything wrong with that?"

"I just wondered why."

"Because it was a nice night."

She got up and poured me a cup of coffee, then took the half-and-half from the refrigerator and handed it to me. "Of course, you always walk in the moonlight."

It was time to steer her off course. "With Jessie you don't always have a choice."

She sipped her coffee, sighing contentedly as the steam rose in her face. "Amen to that."

I took a drink of coffee and pushed my chair away from the table.

"Where are you going?" she asked.

"Out."

"You haven't finished your breakfast."

I grabbed another piece of coffee cake. "I have now."

I left by the back door and started walking toward Woody's. It was a glorious morning, frosty and still, the air clean and sharp, as the trees caught the sun's first rays and sent them shimmering back at me.

As a sometimes writer, I'd tried a hundred times to stuff all the beauty of fall into a poem or a paragraph, and every time I'd come up short. It was like trying to photograph the Grand Canyon at sunset. There was just too much there to ever capture all of it. So you clicked the shutter, took what you could, and hoped you would live long enough to see it again.

At the edge of town I left the road and cut across a pasture toward a woods. It was strange to hear the grass crunch under my feet and look back and see my footprints following. And lonely. A preview of winter.

I smiled to myself. Ever since I'd known Diana, my winters had been anything but lonely. When the nights got too long, I could always count on her for a fire and a bourbon and a couple of hours of warm conversation. And this winter, now that her husband, Fran, had died and she was alone too, I was counting on her for more.

But the fates, or whatever it is that rules our lives, had decided differently. So she was now in Madison, working on a Masters in broadcast journalism. I had one I'd give her. In fact, I'd give her both my degrees, if only she'd come back to Oakalla and stay.

Not to be. Not for a long time anyway. She'd been in Fran's shadow for most of her life and was now determined to make her own mark on the world. That was the difference between us. In trying to make my mark, I'd put a dent in my soul. One that took the last five and a half years to hammer out. Now that I knew who I was, what I wanted, and where I wanted to be, now that I was finally ready for her, she wasn't ready for me. Where are the clowns?

Woody's red Ford pickup was in the drive. But when I knocked on his door, no one answered. All the lights were still on. I went down to the barn and went inside. As I did, I thought I heard the back door close. "Woody?" I called. No answer.

I noticed the doors of the Cadillac were open. They hadn't been last night. Nor were the seats moved out of place, as they were now. Several possibilities, none of which I liked, ran through my mind. I decided the first thing I should do was to get help.

I walked back to the house and made a couple of phone calls. The first one was to Pete Hammond. The second was to Rupert Roberts, sheriff of Adams County, and outside of Ruth the best friend I'd ever had.

Within the hour Pete arrived in his flatbed. Pete had smoked his cigarette down to the filter but seemed not to notice. He was too intent on getting in and getting out of here.

"This is the last time, Garth," he said. "The last time I'm moving that Cadillac anyplace. You change your mind again, and you'll have to get someone else."

"I didn't change my mind. Woody changed his."

"Be that as it may, that Cadillac's taking its last ride on my truck. Now where do you want me to take it?"

I hadn't even thought of that. "Take it to Edgar's. He'll somehow make room for it."

"You sure? He didn't have much room yesterday."

"I'm sure. Tell him to call me if he doesn't."

"Okay. But come hell or high water, I'm leaving it there. You can believe me when I say it."

"I believe you, Pete. Now, what's it going to cost me?"

"Fifty. On top of the other fifty you owe me."

"It's only two miles."

"If you think that's too steep, you can always get somebody else." He threw down his cigarette. He was already reaching for the door.

"How about thirty-five."

"It's fifty. Or nothing."

"Okay, it's fifty." I shook my head. Already I was out a hundred dollars, and I hadn't even shined that first hubcap. The Cadillac was proving more expensive than I thought.

A few minutes later we had the Cadillac loaded on the flatbed and ready to go back to town. As I watched Pete leave, I thought about the light-hearted moment I'd had when I found the Cadillac three days ago. Not so today. Today there was a knot in my stomach and a slow-awakening feeling of dread.

I went back inside the barn. Nothing had been done

on Paul Black's tractor since Sunday, the day I brought Woody the Cadillac. The part we'd been working on still lay where he'd left it. The socket wrench lay beside it. That wasn't like Woody. He was very loyal to Paul. Also, he had a one track mind, and once he fastened on something, he didn't let go until he was through with it.

I didn't see Wilmer Wiemer until I nearly stepped right on top of his new cowboy boots. "Howdy, Garth. How's life treating you?" Small and dapper, not an inch over five feet, Wilmer had silver hair and a patent leather smile that he flashed at every opportunity. He was owner of Oakalla Savings and Loan, the Best Deal Real Estate Company, and everything else in and about Oakalla he could get his hands on. He reminded me of the Susan B. Anthony dollar—small and bright and cute, but mostly copper on the inside.

"Morning, Wilmer. What brings you out this way?"

His smile had dollar signs. He loved to make a buck. "Business as usual."

"I suppose you're calling in another loan?"

He laughed. "No, no, nothing like that. I just came by to make a fair offer on a piece of property."

"What property is that?"

He was still smiling, though he showed more teeth than smile. "I guess that'd be my business, wouldn't it?"

"I guess it would at that, Wilmer."

"You mind if I have a look around?"

"Be my guest."

He walked around the barn, humming to himself as he went. He didn't appear to be looking for anything in particular, but then with Wilmer you never knew. I always suspected that his golden smile hid a pirate's heart.

He stopped when he reached the place where the Cadillac had been. He ceased humming as well, as his shrewd trader eyes took in the rest of the barn, particularly noting the tractor and its parts lying about.

"Woody around?" he asked.

"I haven't seen him."

"Looks like he's got enough to do."

"Looks like it, doesn't it?"

"It's not like him to not be doing it," he said.

"No. It isn't."

"You have any idea where he is?"

"No. Your guess is as good as mine."

"His truck's outside."

"I know. But Woody isn't."

"Well, no sense hanging around here then." He clasped my shoulder on his way past. "Don't take any wooden nickels."

I watched him climb into his dark-green Lincoln Continental and drive away and wondered what he was doing here. One thing was sure. He wasn't just passing the time.

I walked through the barn, out the back door, and down the hill behind it. The leaves were scuffed, like someone had been walking here recently. I came to Stony Creek, appropriately named for its rock bed, which wound its way through a deep hollow. I surprised a pair of wood ducks who rose as one from the creek, flashed brown and teal, and disappeared into the sun.

Sitting beside the creek, I watched a sycamore leaf float lazily downstream. First on Stony Creek, then on the Wisconsin River, then on the Mississippi, if nothing stopped it, it would someday float to the Gulf of Mexico. Today I wished I could go with it.

A minnow swam by and was soon joined by several others. Not deep to begin with, Stony Creek was at low pool, and I could see all the way to the bottom. Something looked like a snake lurking there, though the minnows took no notice of it. Then I reconsidered. It wasn't moving for one thing and for another it looked too stiff to be a snake. Besides no self-respecting snake would be out so early on a frosty morning. It'd freeze its tail off.

A stick then, I decided. Exept it didn't look like a stick

either. I couldn't talk myself out of it. I finally took off my shoes and socks, rolled up my pants legs, and went in after it. I was right. It wasn't a stick. It was a wrecking bar.

I climbed back up the hill. Rupert's patrol car was parked beside Jessie. I hadn't heard him drive by. He must've come from the other way.

"What do you have there?" he asked.

"A wrecking bar."

"I can see that. Where did you find it?"

"Over the hill in Stony Creek."

He took it from me and examined it. "It hasn't been there long," he said. "The rust wipes right off."

"I noticed."

"You think it's Woody's?"

"I wouldn't bet against it."

We went inside the barn to the far wall where Woody kept most of his tools. If he was nothing else, Woody was organized. There was a place for everything, and everything was in its place. Except the wrecking bar. The two brackets that it fit perfectly were empty. "What do you think?" I asked Rupert.

"I think it's Woody's." He went along the wall, examining Woody's tools. He stopped in front of a shovel. "What have we here?"

"It looks like a shovel," I said.

"Some days you amaze even me," he answered. He scraped a piece of dirt from the blade of the shovel and handed it to me. The dirt wasn't yet completely dry. "Looks like Woody's been doing some digging lately."

"Looks like it."

"You have any idea why?"

"No." Though I wished I did.

Together we searched the rest of the barn. Together we came up empty. We went outside into the sunlight where Rupert took a plug of tobacco from his pouch and stuck it in his mouth, then stood for a long time without saying anything. He usually looked somber, but today he looked more somber than usual, like the burden of responsibility he always carried had suddenly shifted and settled in his bones.

"You have any idea where he went?" he asked.

"No. Hasn't anybody seen him in town?"

"Not to my knowledge. I've got Clarkie asking around." He spat in the direction of the barn. "How did you happen to know he was missing?"

"I came by last night, then again this morning. He wasn't here either time. But the way it looked last night, I thought he'd just stepped out and would be back any minute. That's why I waited for him."

"For how long?"

"A couple hours. Maybe more."

"No sign of him?"

"No. I even called a couple of times, but he didn't answer. I did hear a car come out the dead end road and onto Crick Road. It had its lights off part of the way."

"It could've been kids. They park up there a lot. You can't see the ground for the beer cans."

"It could've been. There's something else, though. Last night Woody's pickup was gone. Today it's here."

"What do you make of that?"

"I don't know what to make of it."

"When you do, let me know."

I walked him to his patrol car. Today even his step seemed heavier than usual. "Something bothering you, Rupert?"

"Nothing you can help me with. Somewhere in the county, he thinks around Colburn, a private pilot thought he saw some marijuana growing in a corn field. That was in August. He didn't bother to tell me until two days ago. Now he can't locate it. On top of that you tell me Woody's missing. So instead of spending my time looking for him, which I'd rather do, I've got to chase around the county looking for a patch of marijuana, trying to keep it out of the hands of kids, which is the next thing to impossible anyway. If I burn out this patch, they'll grow another one someplace else—in Colombia or Mexico or the next county over, someplace I can't touch. So what's the gain when it's all said and done?"

"Maybe a job well done."

"Thanks, Garth. But I wasn't looking for a handout. I knew when I took this job the times were changing. It just seems like it gets a little harder every year for me to keep up with them."

"But you will keep an eye out for Woody?"

"I'll do what I can when I can, and when I know for sure he's missing, I'll try to do more."

"That's good enough for me."

He nodded, though it wasn't good enough for him. Then he started the car and drove away, taking the wrecking bar with him.

As I watched him go, I felt my skin draw tight and the hairs on the back of my neck start to tingle. It was almost a sixth sense. Without fail it told me when someone was watching me, or at least I thought someone was. I turned around, saw only the woods and the bright colors of fall. I felt foolish, but still the feeling didn't go away.

I went inside Woody's house. It was cool and stale. At one end of the room was a small sink where Woody's dishes sat soaking in a pan of greasy water. In the middle was a pot-bellied wood stove that had gone cold in the night. At the other end was Woody's unmade bed, his once white sheets now a dirty green.

Beside his bed on the floor was a large pink poodle with a faded blue ribbon around its neck that said, "Won at Frank's." It told me a lot about Woody, perhaps even more about myself. I picked it up and dusted it off with my hand. It seemed a metaphor for all of the lost loves of the world—that if you searched each and every household, somewhere within it would be a reminder of the one that got away, a photograph, a theater ticket stub, a letter stuffed under sweaters in a chest under a bed. The one you once remembered with a flushed face and a thumping heart. The one you now remembered with a smile and a shrug.

I set the poodle down. I could see Woody carrying it around the county fair under the admiring glances of all those who weren't carrying one. It must've been a big day for him. Now here it sat in a dumpy little room collecting dust. While Woody sat where? Better I didn't think about it, or I'd really cheer myself up.

I turned off the lights and started to leave when I saw a worn piece of paper sticking out from under Woody's phone. A faded phone number along with several scribbles were written on it. The scribbles looked like mine when I couldn't get a pen to write. The number was a local number. Not an Oakalla number, but one you could dial without charge. Just for the hell of it, I dialed it. It was busy. I folded the piece of paper, stuck it into my shirt pocket, and promptly forgot about it.

Outside I stopped at Woody's pickup long enough to check it out. The keys were in the ignition, where he always kept them. I looked in the bed and found nothing unusual. Just an assortment of Woody's junk, a spare tire, and an old lug wrench that looked too rusty to be of much use. It reminded me of Jessie's trunk, except his spare tire had air in it.

5

I ate lunch at the Corner Bar and Grill—a cheeseburger with fried onions and a glass of milk. Sometime today I had to get started on Friday's edition of the *Oakalla Reporter.*

I could handle the nuts and bolts okay—the who did what when and to whom—but lately I'd had real trouble writing my weekly column. It seemed like everything I wrote, I'd written before. I hadn't. It just seemed that way. And if it seemed that way to me, it probably seemed that way to my readers too.

This week I wanted to do something different. The problem was I also wanted to look for Woody. I couldn't do both. Or could I? I smiled. Rupert was right. Sometimes I *was* amazing.

Sniffy Smith had been a barber for as long as I could remember. He had his shop right next to the hardware, between it and the Corner Bar and Grill, for over forty years until he'd retired two years ago. On Fridays he'd still come into the shop and help his son-in-law with the overflow, but he spent most of his time loafing and talking sports at the Marathon Gas Station.

He was there today, perched on his favorite stool where he could watch the drive and talk at the same time. I didn't know what his first name was. He'd always been Sniffy to me. Sniffy to everyone else, too, since he had the habit of sniffing in your ear as he cut your hair, probably to keep the hair out of his nose. He was drowsing now, letting his head droop in the sun. Small and plump, with the softest hands I'd ever felt on a man, Sniffy never was one to spend much time out-of-doors. A lot of Oakalla's residents looked like they'd been chiseled from its rocky earth itself. Sniffy, on the other hand, looked like he'd come in a bag of marshmallows.

Sniffy's eyes opened, and he righted himself as I came in the door. Then he smiled a greeting. Against my better judgment, Sniffy was still my barber. I always got my hair cut on Fridays.

"Afternoon, Sniffy," I said.

"Afternoon, Garth. What are you up to?"

"As little as possible."

Sniffy laughed. "Join the crowd. If I did any less, I wouldn't even need a shadow." Then he laughed some more. That's what I liked about Sniffy. He wasn't hard to please. He cut hair the same way. Off the ear, over the ear, down to the skin, or down to your navel, it was all the same to him. You told him what to cut and he cut it. Where you got in trouble was when you left it up to him.

I took the stool beside him. It did feel good there in the sun, good enough to understand why Sniffy camped there. "Been here long?" I asked.

"Nearly two years now," he answered.

"I mean today."

"Since about ten."

"Sounds like you got a late start."

"I did. I overslept. First time in a week. Must be old age creeping up on me."

"Must be," I agreed.

He noticed I had a pen and notebook with me. "What's that for?"

"I'm doing interviews."

"What about?"

"Marijuana."

"You mean for and against it?"

"Something like that. I'm interested in what the people of Oakalla think about its use, whether the laws ought to be tougher or easier, or if we should have any laws at all."

"Well, what do they think so far?" he asked.

"I don't know. You're my first customer."

"Well, you sure picked a dandy to start with," he said. "I don't even smoke or chew. Drink some. But never before five. What I know about marijuana wouldn't fill a matchbook, let alone that thing you're carrying."

"You don't have to be an expert. I want to know what *you* feel about it, not what you read somewhere."

"I don't have to be right?"

"I'd rather you weren't."

"Okay." Sniffy sat up a little straighter. "I feel we ought to legalize the damn stuff, then give it away, like they do the cheese and butter to us senior citizens. That way nobody'd want it. Hell, I've got a whole freezer full of cheese at home that nobody wants, not even Sarah Sue Richardson, and she'll take anything, even week-old chicken bones. I could fill my freezer full of marijuana just as well. Save us taxpayers a lot of money in the bargain."

"How's that, Sniffy?"

He was almost indignant now. "Why it's as plain as the nose on your face! If it's free, people don't want it. Put a price on it and they do. The higher the price, the more they want it. It's Newton's Fifth Law of Economics. I know. I read that much somewhere. So instead of paying all these

46

people to try to stamp out the damn stuff . . . which they'll never do. How can they, when anyone of us can grow it in our back yard? So instead of paying all these people to stamp it out, we pay farmers to grow it. Then give it away to the needy." He folded his arms and looked wise. "Kills two birds with one stone, the way I see it. Gets it off the street and helps out the farmer at the same time. Besides that, since it don't cost anything, you don't have to steal anything to buy it. And since crooks can't make any money on it, there ain't no sense in pushing it the way they do. Hell, you never heard of organized crime before Prohibition. But no, somebody had to go out and save us from ourselves! Like those do-gooder ministers on TV! If you really want to get me started, why don't you ask me about them!"

"Thanks, Sniffy. Maybe later."

He was rolling now. He'd even attracted a small audience—fellow loafers who'd put aside their cribbage game for the moment. I'd never seen Sniffy on a soap box before. Neither had anyone else from the look on their faces. Best of all, Sniffy was right at home there. "Anything else you want to know?" he asked.

"No. I think that'll do for now."

"You don't really believe that shit?" Zeke Clodfelter asked from behind me. "If we was to do what Sniffy says, the whole country'd be drug addicts. Everyone under thirty anyhow."

"Who says?" Sniffy answered.

"I say," Zeke replied. "Hell, we got ten-year-old kids on the stuff now. If it was legal and *free,* which is even worse, they'd be putting it on their breakfast cereal, right there on top their Peanut Butter Captain Crunch! Now wouldn't that be a fine mess!"

I looked at the door. I wondered if I could get out of here before the shooting started. Too late. "What do you think, Garth?" somebody asked.

"Today I'm not interested in what I think," I said. "I'm

interested in what you think. After I hear from all of you, I'll give my opinion in the *Reporter*."

"We plan to hold you to it. A lot of us would like to know."

"I'm no expert," I tried to point out. "Mine is just one man's opinion, the same as yours. It doesn't count for any more or any less."

"But you're smarter than the rest of us," Sniffy said. "Even if you hadn't been to college."

I didn't know how to answer that, so I didn't try. In some ways I was smarter than the rest of them, in some ways I wasn't. It depended on the question.

I walked to the door and stopped. "By the way, have any of you seen Woody Padgett around lately?"

"Why? Is he missing?" Sniffy asked.

"Why do you ask?"

"Wilmer Wiemer was just in here asking about him."

That was something I hadn't counted on. Leave it to Wilmer to muddy the water. "He might be missing," I answered. "I'm just trying to find out if he is."

"Well, it's like we told Wilmer. We haven't seen Woody since Monday forenoon, when he was in here having his oil changed. I think he filled up with gas, too, didn't he, Zeke?"

Zeke nodded. "And bought a case of Coke and a box of Snickers. We asked him if he was going on a trip and Woody just smiled. You know Woody. It's hard to pin him down on anything."

"Which way did Woody go from here?" I asked. "Does anybody remember?"

"He went north," Sniffy said. "Up Fair Haven Road."

"Did anybody see him come back?"

They shook their heads. No one had. I thanked them and left.

From there I went to the market, then the drug store, then the bank, hardware, post office, and five and dime. Everyone had an opinion on marijuana. No one had seen

48

Woody. Except Fritz Gascho at the hardware said he thought he saw Woody's pickup go by heading west and for home. He said it was hard to miss Woody's truck. I agreed with him. He also said something else that interested me. He said Wilmer Wiemer had been in earlier looking for Woody.

It was after five when I got home. Ruth was puttering around the kitchen, looking busy. But so far I couldn't see much progress toward supper. I took a seat at the kitchen table and hoped I wouldn't be in her way.

"Any phone calls?" I asked.

"No phone calls," she answered. "At least not from Diana."

"Just thought I'd ask."

"It never hurts to ask."

"I saw Wilmer Wiemer today at Woody's," I said.

"What about it?"

"He said he was there to make a purchase."

"He probably was. You know Wilmer. He never misses a trick. He's been after that piece of property for the last ten years. Now that another year's passed, he probably figures that Paul Black will sell it to him."

"Paul Black wasn't there. I was."

"Wilmer didn't know that."

"Then again he might not have been talking about the property."

"What else would he be interested in? Wilmer doesn't drill many dry holes."

I knew one thing he might be interested in. The same thing I was interested in—the Cadillac. "I don't know," I said. "I don't even know why he's after that property, do you?"

"No. It's his best kept secret. Paul Black even hired some geologists to look it over. They said there wasn't anything there worth digging for."

"So why doesn't Paul Black sell it?"

"You'll have to ask him. My guess is Woody. After

living there for most of his life, Woody's come to think of it as his own."

"What if Woody left?" I asked her.

"What if he did?"

"Do you think Paul would sell it then?"

"Hard to figure," she said. "If he did, I might try to buy it myself."

"What would you do with it?"

"The same thing Woody does with it. Garden and raise bees and grow apples and fish when I had a mind to. It's not a bad life, not a bad life at all."

"You almost sound envious."

"I am," she said. "After spending most of my life on the farm, it's hard to depend on somebody else. It used to be I had God or me to blame when I had to do without. Now it's the stock boy at Kroger's or whoever it is that orders the damn stuff they're always out of. Who's in charge? I used to know. I'm not sure I do anymore. And I can't say I like it. Do you?"

I shook my head. "No. I've had some of the same thoughts myself."

"The times are changing."

"That's what Rupert says."

"What's he up to these days?" she asked.

"He's looking for a field of marijuana over around Colburn. A private pilot spotted it from the air."

"I wish him luck. There's a lot of empty space over there."

"That there is." I thought about it a moment, then decided to ask her. "Would you do me a favor?"

"Depends on what it is."

"See if you can find out why Wilmer's interested in that farm where Woody lives. I'll work on it from my end too."

"What business is that of yours?"

"I'm just curious. There might be a story in it."

50

"Are you sure it's not more than that? Wilmer never has been your favorite person."

"That's true. Still, he seems to like me. I can't figure it out."

"Why waste time trying?"

"You might have a point."

After supper I laid in some wood and built a fire in the fireplace. Listening to it crackle and pop, feeling its warmth seep into me and take away the evening chill, I was reminded how much I liked a fire, how much I'd missed one lately.

Ruth sat in her favorite chair reading a magazine. I sat on the hearth, looking at the ceiling, watching the fire dance shadows across it. I should have been at ease. I wasn't. Too many unanswered questions were running through my mind.

For the past fifty years or so Woody Padgett had been a fixture in Oakalla, as predictable as the four seasons. Now suddenly he was missing—the day after I'd entrusted the Cadillac to him. And the day after that Wilmer Wiemer was suddenly interested in something inside Woody's barn and then in finding Woody himself. Either it was a hell of a coincidence or there was something about that Cadillac that somebody had forgotten to tell me. I decided to go to the source to find out.

Ruth peered over her magazine and gave me a questioning look. "Why do you want to know?"

"I'm just curious, that's all."

"What was your question again?" She returned to the magazine.

"Why do you want a Cadillac? Specifically, why a 1936 Cadillac convertible?"

"Why not a Cadillac?"

"I don't know. It just doesn't seem your style."

She laid the magazine down. "Go on." She wasn't trying to make it easy for me.

"That's all. It just doesn't seem your style."

"You mean you never thought I was a snob?"

"That's about it."

"I didn't either. Until I saw it for the first time."

"When was that?"

"July 1936. I was a barefoot bride at the time. I mean that. We were so poor I couldn't even afford shoelaces, let alone shoes. It was in the evening right about sundown. I was just coming up from milking, carrying a pail in each hand up to the separator. And it was hot. It must've been a hundred in the shade that day, and I'd helped feed at least twenty threshers for dinner. Then had to clean up after them. So here I was, little more than a child, doing a woman's work, with all a woman's aches and pains. Married besides—to a stranger it seemed, though I'd known him all my life. And I didn't think I was going to make it through the day, let alone a lifetime. Then here came Clinton Bass driving up in that Cadillac. He was just out driving around, killing time. He told me to get in. He'd take me for a ride. I asked what about the milk. He said if it spoiled he'd pay me for it. It was too damn hot for a pretty girl like me to be lugging two pails of milk around like a plow horse. And he'd tell Karl that the next time he saw him. If he did, it was the first time anyone told Karl anything. Anyway, I set the milk down, got in that Cadillac, and went for a ride. I can't describe the feeling. But the shadows were long and cool, all the smells of summer right there in our faces, as we went zipping along like we owned the world, which we did at that moment. I never wanted to come back. But when we did an hour later, I knew I was going to make it. Through the day at least. And maybe the day after that." She smiled at me. One of her rare and gentle smiles. "That's why."

"Do you know whatever happened to the Cadillac?"

"No. Clinton Bass had it for several years, but most of the time it just sat in his garage. He had a stroke about a year after he bought it, and about the best he could do after that was to drive it uptown and back. Then Doc

Airhart owned it for a time, and after that I lost track of it. I guess it moved out of town."

"You say Doc Airhart owned it?" He hadn't told me that.

"I'm sure he did. I remember seeing him riding around town in it. He cut quite a figure in those days. He and that Cadillac were a hard combination to beat."

"I imagine they were. Thanks, Ruth."

"You haven't seen one, have you?" She was hopeful.

"No. I was just curious."

She picked up her magazine and started reading. "Too bad."

Why did I think she knew more than she let on?

6

The fire was nearly out. I was alone in the house. Ruth had left to play auction bridge with some of her old cronies, and she'd taken Jessie, since her Volkswagen was in the shop with a bad coil. I knew it was a mistake to pair those two. Only grief ever came of it. But sometimes I just couldn't resist the temptation.

I watched the fire burn down to ashes, drawing closer as it cooled. A fire was like a whisper: the softer it was, the closer you wanted to be. I remembered the night Diana and I made love on the floor in front of her fireplace, then, as I had tonight, watched the fire fall and die. It seemed then that we had a thousand fires ahead of us. Now we were down to nine hundred ninety-nine. If I built one tomorrow night, nine hundred ninety-eight. And who knew how many we'd have left at winter's end? Time went on, with or without the one you loved. Some counted the days. I counted the fires.

I closed the damper and walked to the Corner Bar and Grill. I decided to have a beer or two, then walk up to Edgar's and look in on him. I didn't want him to go the way of Woody.

Doc Airhart was sitting at the bar, drinking Scotch on the rocks. He once told me that drinking it any other way was a crime against humanity—punishable by death or that failing, a year in a fast food restaurant.

I took a seat beside him. "Evening, Doc," I said.

"Evening, Garth. You get your Cadillac?"

"I got it."

"Where is it now?"

"Edgar's."

"I thought you took it to Woody's."

"Who told you that?"

"It's a small town. Word gets around."

"I did take it to Woody's. He decided not to work on it."

"Why not?"

"You'll have to ask him."

He took a drink of his Scotch, savoring every drop. "I would if I could find him."

"I didn't know you were looking."

"I wasn't. As I said, word gets around."

Hiram, the bartender, came, and I ordered a beer. "You might've told me you once owned the Cadillac," I said.

Doc seemed to sink further into his Scotch. "What good would that have done?"

"I don't know. It might explain what you have against it."

"Who said I have anything against it?"

"Come off it, Doc. You haven't been yourself since the minute we found it."

He wouldn't look at me. He continued to stare into his glass. "Neither will you be for long, if you keep it."

"What's that supposed to mean?"

"Let sleeping dogs lie, Garth. It's good advice. About the best my father ever gave me. I'm giving it to you, no charge."

"Why? What are you telling me?"

"I'm telling you to let well enough alone. You don't know where that Cadillac's been, what strings might still be attached to it."

"Just walk away and leave it?"

"Walk or drive, whatever's handy."

I studied him. He was dead serious. "Why?" I repeated.

But he didn't answer. Instead he got up and walked to the side door that led out of the bar onto Jackson Street. He stood there a moment, then turned back to me. "At Edgar's, you say?"

"What's that?"

"The Cadillac's at Edgar's now?"

"Yes."

"Then somebody ought to warn him."

"I plan to stop by there later."

"See that you do. The sooner the better."

"Don't be so damned melancholy! It's just a car, for God's sake! Not a bomb!"

That really ruffled his feathers. "Don't be so damned sure! Don't be so God damned sure!" He left, slamming the door behind him.

I waited for my beer, drank it slowly, and left by the side door also. I walked east, then north on Fair Haven Road toward Edgar's. I believed Doc had overstated his case, but at the same time I didn't want to take any chances.

I stopped outside the overhead door of the shop and listened for a moment. I heard a rustle inside, like a mouse busy building a nest. I walked around to the side door, looked through the window, and saw a fire. It wasn't moving, but crouched in the far corner just waiting for air.

56

The Cadillac sat less than three feet away, glowing eerily in the fire's light, as if the fire were already upon it.

I ran for Edgar's house and help. Edgar was still up, sitting in his pajamas at the kitchen table drinking coffee.

"Garth, is that you?" He squinted at me with his good eye as I slammed open the back door.

"I need a fire extinguisher! You have one?"

He thought a moment. "Someplace. Look in the shop on the right hand side just after you clear the door."

"Thanks." I was on my way.

"What's up?"

"Fire!"

I looked inside at the fire. It was still crouched where I left it. But once it started to spread, it would go in a hurry.

I took a deep breath, held it, and went inside. The fire roared to life as I did. I fumbled for the light switch but couldn't find it. Nor could I find the fire extinguisher. But the way Edgar kept house, a circus could be hiding in here and I'd never see it.

I took a quick breath, mostly of smoke, and began to rummage through a pile of junk on the floor. I cut my hand on a piece of steel and momentarily lost control as junk went rattling off the walls like machine gun flack. But no fire extinguisher. I wheeled and started for the fire, intending to stomp it out if nothing else, and nearly ran headlong into Edgar. He brushed past me, turned on the light, and reached for the fire extinguisher in the same motion. There it hung in plain sight, against the wall on the right hand side of the door where he said it would be.

He didn't waste any time. He pulled the pin and had the fire out within seconds. Then he began to wheeze, as he dropped the extinguisher and stumbled for the door. I helped him outside where he sat on the ground. In a few minutes he was breathing normally again.

We opened both doors and the one window of the shop to air it out. The fire had started in the corner in a pile of oily rags. It could have been spontaneous combustion. But I didn't think so. Judging by the scowl on his face, neither did Edgar.

"What do you think?" I asked.

"I think I wish your Cadillac was someplace else," he said. "This shop ain't much, but I'd sure hate to try to replace everything that's in it."

"Do you want me to move it someplace else?" I asked.

"No, I want you to get rid of it. Take it back where it came from, wherever that is. It's bad business, Garth. That car is bad business."

"Says who?"

"Says me. Says Woody if he were still around to tell you."

"You think Woody's in trouble?"

"What do you think, Garth? You know Woody. When was the last time he went off and didn't tell anybody? In early spring maybe, when the wanderlust got to him and the fields were still too wet to work. But not in the middle of harvest season, not with Paul Black depending on him. And not with your Cadillac and Paul Black's tractor setting there in his barn."

"But why would anyone harm him?"

"Why would anyone set fire to my place? You figure it out."

"The Cadillac?"

"What else? Woody had it a day and he's missing. I've had it less than a day and my shop damn near burned down. Now I ain't real bright, but I'm bright enough to figure that out. Any way you look at it, that Cadillac is bad business."

"Do you want me to move it?" I repeated.

"Where to? You're running out of places." Satisfied that the fire was out, he pulled down the overhead door and locked it. "If you want to keep it here, I'll keep it here and work on it in my spare time. But as soon as it's ready, it's going. I don't care if it's Ruth's birthday or not."

"I can help you with it if you want," I said as a peace offering.

"Where are you going to find the time to do that? You meet yourself going and coming the way it is."

He had a point. Already it was Tuesday going on Wednesday. By Thursday at this time I had to have the *Oakalla Reporter* ready to print.

"You're right, Edgar. But I think I'll spend tonight at least. Caddysit if nothing else."

"Do as you like. I'm going to bed."

I stopped him before he got away. "You didn't by chance see somebody out here, did you?"

"Nope. Not a soul."

"Night, Edgar."

"Night, Garth. If you get lonely, I'll have a pot of coffee on the stove."

I looked for someplace to sit and found a soft patch of grass in the shadow of Edgar's cedar. It was comfortable there on the ground, neither as damp nor as cool as I expected, even though the sky had cleared and the moon was round and white. I spent a few minutes star-gazing, trying to guess which star was which and trying to find the Little Dipper. All in vain.

I heard a leaf crunch underfoot. The sound came from somewhere behind me. It seemed like the next yard north. I slowly turned to look, saw nothing but houses, bushes, and trees, and a street light at the edge of town. I looked up and down Fair Haven Road and saw nothing there either.

Standing up, I saw something that startled me. A quarter mile away, outlined by the light of the moon, the old Brainard mansion sat upon a knob. From where I was standing, it looked like a light was burning upstairs. But it wasn't a light. It was only the moon reflecting on the window, that looked like a light. It sent a shiver down my spine. The Brainard mansion had been vacant for the past thirty years.

Suddenly I was cool. I decided to move. I walked into the yard north and found a half-eaten apple lying on the ground. I looked around. I didn't see any apple trees close by.

I examined the apple. Its meat was still white. It couldn't have been here long. I walked around to the back of the house, but didn't find a tree that matched the apple. I carried it into the moonlight for a better look at it. Then I tasted it to make sure. It was what Grandmother Ryland called a Golden Pippin, the best-tasting apple I'd ever eaten. There weren't many Golden Pippin apple trees growing in Oakalla. In fact, the only one I knew of grew right next to the Brainard mansion.

I heard someone on the sidewalk coming my way. By the sound of his footsteps, he was in a hurry. He was hitting the sidewalk hard, heels clicking every step. I waited for him to pass, then stepped out into the street to get a better look at him. He was dressed all in black, and his head floated like a silver balloon in and out of the shadows. Wilmer Wiemer was on his way home. But I wondered where he'd been. Business, as usual?

7

Ruth and I sat across from each other at the breakfast table. She hadn't spoken to me all morning and judging by the set in her jaw, planned to keep her silence for at least the next millennium. Meanwhile I was gagging on a bowl of her oatmeal wishing she'd leave the room so I could run it down the disposal. But mother hen that she was, she'd see that I ate it even if it killed me—which I believe was her plan all along.

"Look," I said to break the ice, "I didn't know Jessie's tire was going to go flat. Besides, you've changed flat tires before." I'd met her coming in the door at three A.M. She was beyond words. A first for her.

"It wasn't the flat on the left front I minded so much," she said. "It was the one in the trunk—the one buried under God knows how many years of your junk. . . ." She was gathering steam now. I was in for the whole nine yards. "The one that looked like it had been thrown off a

61

cliff, run through a saw mill, then used for target practice by the entire Sioux Nation! The one that had so many holes in it you couldn't have patched it with the Goodyear Blimp! I know. I rolled it a mile into town to find out. Where did you get it anyway, steal it off somebody's pier?"

"It was an original. You know how I hate to throw things away." I pushed the oatmeal aside and took a drink of coffee. It wasn't much better. "By the way, where is Jessie? I didn't see her when I came in last night."

"Right at the top of Dead Man's Hill—in neutral with the emergency brake off."

"It doesn't matter. The emergency brake never worked anyway."

"When are you going to break down and buy a new car?"

"When Jessie finally breaks down for good, whenever that is."

Ruth looked at her watch. "I'd say within the hour or however long it takes to carry a sledgehammer out there."

"Have a heart, Ruth. You and she have a lot in common."

"I'll pretend I didn't hear that. The only thing we have in common is aggravation. A problem I'm about to correct."

"But you will have her back by sundown?"

"What's the matter with you, your legs broken?"

"No. They'll be walking in other directions."

"Such as?"

"Here and there. You know me."

"Enough to know better than to ask."

Outside, the chill of morning still hung in the shadows, but the sun was warm on my face and the deep blue of the sky promised another beautiful day. I walked north along Fair Haven Road toward the Brainard mansion. At the edge of town I stopped to watch Thelma Osterday beat her rug, as the dust from it rose in a cloud that hung over her clothesline like a thunderhead.

Though a decade younger, Thelma reminded me a lot of Ruth. She had blond hair, broad shoulders, rosy cheeks, and a jaw like the Rock of Gibraltar. And like Ruth, she'd seen her share of trouble. She was married and widowed within a year—to a local war hero, Frank Osterday, who died when an old piece of shrapnel moved and cut an artery in his brain. She'd never remarried, but continued to live alone here at the north edge of Oakalla. She'd told me this in patches of conversation we'd had over the past five years. She'd also hinted there was an old flame still burning in her. Though she didn't say for whom.

"Nice day," I offered.

"What's nice about it?" With sharp bold strokes she was applying the coup de grace to the rug.

"It could be raining."

She stopped long enough to glare at me. "I suppose it could be. But it ain't."

"You have a point." I nodded and started on. Normally Thelma and I saw eye-to-eye.

"I'm sorry, Garth. I ain't in the mood to shoot the bull. Last night at sundown someone stole my comforter right off this line. My best one, too, and with winter coming on." Then she muttered something I didn't hear.

"What was that?" I asked.

"Nothing. It ain't possible."

"What isn't possible?"

"If it ain't possible, it ain't possible, is it?"

"No, I guess not." I walked on.

The Brainard mansion sat by itself back a long, wide lane just north of town. Anchored on both sides by huge jack and red oaks that now burned with a dull red flame in the morning sun, the lane was overgrown with weeds and brush and showed the neglect of the past thirty years.

But it wasn't as bad as it could have been. Someone, who many in Oakalla thought was the ghost of Colonel Brainard himself, kept the place in some semblance of repair. Though several had heard him at his work late at night, no one that I knew had ever actually seen him—only the results of his labors. They couldn't be denied. Otherwise, the lane would have been a woods and the mansion a pile of bricks by now.

No one had lived here since Nellie Brainard, Colonel Brainard's widow, had left for parts unknown over thirty years ago. Some said she'd finally found Colonel Brainard's fortune that was supposedly buried on this property and was now living somewhere in seclusion. Others said she'd given up looking for the money and had moved on in search of greener pastures. Still others believed the Colonel himself had driven her away with his nightly hauntings. I didn't know. I had my own memories of Nellie, none of which were very clear. Perhaps Ruth could enlighten me.

I remembered Nellie and the Colonel as never having been the ideal couple. Nearly forty years her senior, he'd tried to keep Nellie on a leash as short as the one to his wallet. He never let her go anywhere without him, and when he went out alone, he gave her orders to stay home.

Not one to take orders from anyone, Nellie defied him at every opportunity. She went where she pleased when she pleased and left it up to him to track her down.

That was why it came as a surprise when he was the one who drove off one day and never returned. I barely remember the incident. I couldn't have been more than four at the time. I do remember taking Grandmother Ryland's shovel one day a few years later and walking all the way to the edge of the Brainard estate before my courage gave out on me. I figured if there was money buried there like everyone said, I might as well try to find it.

But the rumors of Colonel Brainard's ghost stopped me. That and the very real presence of Nellie. Earlier that year, she'd made her impression on my very impressionable mind. I hadn't forgotten her to this day. And even now I hesitated, thinking she might be somewhere about.

At lane's end I stopped to stare at the Brainard mansion. Imposing. That was the only way to describe it. Built of dark red bricks that looked like they'd been fired too long, it had a high sheer face and a steep gabled roof that looked too small in proportion to its frame, like the wings of an ostrich. It had no porch or balcony and its windows were high narrow arches that looked like something from a gothic nightmare. No wonder Nellie left. No one in her right mind could live here alone.

I wasn't quite ready to go inside. A few apple trees were growing along the south side of the yard between the mansion and a corn field. I walked over to them. They were spindly and nearly bare of leaves but all bore fruit. I recognized the one in the middle right next to the fence. It was the Golden Pippin I'd climbed as a boy to steal yellow apples. I picked a newly fallen one off the ground and tasted it. Still as sweet and good as ever. Maybe more so when I counted the years between it and my first taste of one.

I walked to the front door of the mansion and stood staring at it like it was the Sphinx. What awaited inside? The ghost of Colonel Brainard? Or maybe Nellie herself? One thing was certain. Whoever looked after the yard also took good care of the house. Not a window was broken or a shingle out of place. The mansion was in remarkably good shape for having stood vacant for over thirty years. I also wondered who had been paying the taxes on it all this time.

I went inside and wished I hadn't. Outside it was warm and bright and ripe with the scent of fall. In here it was cool and dark with a dense dead smell that old buildings have from sitting unused too long.

I was in an anteroom of sorts. It was a high narrow room that had finally begun to show its age. The wallpaper had started to peel, and there was a long deep crack in the plaster ceiling through which plaster sifted a few grains at a time, piling in a snowlike mound on the floor. Austere even in decay, the room reminded me of an old aristocrat, who though bent by arthritis could still look down his nose at you.

I went into the parlor, or what I guessed was the parlor. It was a small square room that had seen much use over the years. Its hardwood floor was scuffed and heavily heel-marked, and there were marks on the walls where furniture had rubbed. The room was bare, however, except for a Victorian love seat that sat facing the wall in a cynical pose. Whoever had put it there, staring endlessly into a blank wall, had picked her last forget-me-not.

I stooped to examine it and let my hand rest on it a moment. Its red velvet cushion was newspaper thin. It felt good to touch—frail and soft and feminine. No cynicism here. Just worn thin over the years until the bones showed through the skin. Worn out by life—like my grandmother Ryland.

The parlor led into a larger room that I guessed was once the dining room. The floor here was barely marked and shone with a dark lustre where I stirred the dust. A spiral staircase led from the east end of the room upstairs. It was made of rosewood and looked too elegant to use.

I hesitated, then started up it. I stopped, blinked, and backed down a step. No, I wasn't seeing things. There *was* a small footprint outlined in the dust on the step. And one on the next step and the next all the way up the stairs. At the top I looked back down. The same footprints led down the stairs.

I had a choice: left down a dark hallway or right down a dark hallway. I went to the right and ducked into the first room I came to. It was a bathroom. The sink was an old-timer with a deep bowl and porcelain handles in the shape of tear drops. No water came out of the faucet. I didn't know why I expected it to.

The next door past the bathroom led me into a

bedroom, and I came face-to-face with the largest bed I'd ever seen. The headboard must have been at least eleven feet high and was made of a dark heavy wood that looked like it belonged to the Amazon. It was carved with the faces of savages, each one more hideous than the last, and the one at the very top of the headboard looked like agony itself. I wondered why it looked familiar. Then I remembered the wood carving my brother had brought back from the Philippines. It was a headhunter carrying a hand-ax in one hand and a head in the other. The face on the head was the same face at the top of the headboard.

I stood for a moment awed by the bed. Then I approached it—to prove to myself I could. The mattress lay four feet off the floor and was covered with a checkerboard comforter.

I slapped the comforter, expecting to see the dust fly. When it didn't, I turned it back and smelled it. It smelled fresh, like it had been aired recently, and not at all like the musty linens beneath it.

I wanted out of here. I couldn't explain why. I just wanted out. I pulled the comforter off the bed, folded it, and started for the door. I stopped. There before me was the portrait of a young woman, so close and vivid I felt I was in her living presence.

She looked no more than eighteen. She was wearing a bright red cap with a bright red bow tied under her chin. Neither looking at me nor away from me but at something only she could see, her eyes were clear and bold, hawklike in their intensity, and her wide thin mouth neither smiled nor frowned, yet somehow hinted mockery.

She had the kind of beauty that made you look, whether you wanted to or not. The kind that some men wanted to possess, just to show off to other men. The kind that shocked you with its frankness, made you pinch yourself in disbelief when you encountered it for the first time, then made you shake your head and wonder when you realized how cheaply it could be had. It was the kind of beauty that Doc and I had talked about on Saturday, the kind that could do whatever it wanted, just because it wanted.

I stood and stared for what seemed like an hour, trying to catch up to the thoughts racing through my mind. Why would a beauty like Nellie marry a man nearly forty years older? A man who treated her badly at that? I could think of only one reason. His money. And why would Colonel Brainard marry an eighteen-year-old girl? A wild one to boot? The answer seemed obvious. Her beauty. So what else was new? It happened every day. But what if the beauty and the money were both extreme? Would that be an everyday happening, especially here in Oakalla where both were equally rare? And would the lovers find hell or paradise?

On my way to the stairs I thought I heard footsteps running through the house. Then I heard a door open and close. I couldn't tell if it was the back or the front. I hurried down the stairs, out the front door and almost collided with a fat man.

He wasn't all that fat, actually. He just looked like it. He had a round bald head, bull-like shoulders, and a thick furry brow that gave him a walrus look. His eyes were small and deep-set, his ears small and red, like they'd been boxed recently. I couldn't tell if he was angry or embarrassed. One thing was certain. He wasn't expecting me to come out the door.

"What are you doing here?" he demanded. He had the voice of authority. He was used to asking the questions.

"I might ask you the same thing. I'm Garth Ryland. I live here in Oakalla. I don't ever remember seeing you around."

"I don't care who you are. You're on my property."

"Since when?" I asked. "You're too young to be Colonel Brainard and not pretty enough to be Nellie. That doesn't leave anybody else that I know of."

He stared at me, his ears growing redder all the while.

He didn't plan to back down. Neither did I. The direction we were headed, we were going to be here until Thanksgiving.

Then he suddenly turned and left, making his own path down the lane and out to the road. I noticed he drove a black Mercedes. I could see it glint in the sun as it went south along Fair Haven Road. Whoever he was and whatever his business, it looked like it had been good to him. At least better than the newspaper business had been to me.

I watched him as far as the city limits sign, then went back inside. I'd heard someone in here before. I wondered if it was he—or someone else.

8

I started back toward town. Thelma Osterday sat on her porch hulling walnuts. She wore gloves to keep the stain off her hands and a look of forebearance that would have put Job to shame. I sometimes wondered about that story, if maybe the teller hadn't got his genders crossed. For it seemed to me, if Ruth and Grandmother Ryland counted for anything, it was the women of the world who suffered longest and hardest and in the end required the most patience. And the men who did were the exception rather than the rule.

"Is this yours?" I asked, laying the comforter beside her.

She glanced at it, then went back to hulling walnuts. "Looks like it. Where did you find it?"

I pointed. "The Brainard mansion. It walked as far as the second floor."

"Figures" was all she said.

70

"Do you have any idea how it got there?"

She continued hulling walnuts. "Some."

"Do you mind explaining that?"

"Yes, Garth, I'm afraid I do." She picked up a pair of gloves and handed them to me. "As long as you're here, you might as well make yourself useful. You do know how, don't you?"

I put on the gloves and began to grind away at the hull. "I know how."

"I thought you did."

We didn't talk for a while. We were both too busy hulling. I remembered my first experience at it. I was in seventh grade, and Dick Davis, my buddy since first grade, and I decided to go gather some walnuts for the winter. So we took a burlap sack, went to the east edge of town where the walnut trees grew, and talked and hulled as we filled the sack. Soon we noticed our hands were very brown. No matter. We thought they looked cool. Woodsman hands. Macho hands. Our mothers were less impressed. So were our classmates, especially the girls, whom we were trying so hard to impress at that age. It didn't matter that the stain wouldn't come off—not even after six scrubbings with turpentine and Lava soap. The girls wouldn't come near us, afraid we'd rub off on them. It was my first real taste of discrimination. Sadly, it wasn't my last.

"You do good work," Thelma finally said.

"Thanks. So do you."

"I mean with your newspaper. If either one of us had to make a living doing this, we'd both starve."

"Thanks again," I said. "It's nice to be appreciated."

"You're welcome. The paper never was much before you came to town. Mainly who did what when and who was going to what when—already old news to most of us. But you put some life in it. Some guts too. I like that. I feel I'm getting my money's worth now. But you have one fault, if you don't mind me saying so."

Only one? That would be news to Ruth. "No, I don't mind. Lay it on me."

"You don't know when to stop."

"I've been told that."

"Well, I'm telling you again. I've got my comforter back. That's all that matters. Let it rest there."

"You saw somebody, didn't you? You saw somebody take your comforter."

"I didn't see anybody." She said it too quickly and with too much force.

"And your comforter flew over there by itself. It's a magic carpet, is that it?"

"That's it. You see? I've given you good advice and you just don't want to take it."

I stared at the Brainard mansion. If only walls could talk.

"What is it now?" she asked.

"Nothing. It just seems strange, that's all."

"What does?"

"The mansion. It's in good shape, a lot better than it should be."

"Meaning?"

"Meaning somebody keeps it that way."

"Who are you suggesting?" she asked. "Big-Ears himself?"

"Big-Ears?"

"Big-Ears Brainard. He wasn't really a colonel. He never even fought in a war. He just called himself that, so other people started calling him that too. It was because he had old money in the family. He'd been poor like the rest of us, it'd been Private Brainard."

"Tell me more."

"What do you want to know?"

"Do you think he haunts the place like they say?"

"I wouldn't bet against it."

I glanced at her. She seemed serious.

"I've heard someone myself," she continued, "ham-

72

mering away in the middle of the night. Not as much anymore but still once or twice a year."

"You're sure it's Big-Ears?"

"Who else would it be?" She asked, though it seemed like she knew.

Good question. "What about Nellie?"

"What about her?"

"Did she really find Big-Ears' money? Or did something else happen to her?"

She gave me a hard look. "Like what?"

"I was hoping you could tell me."

"I can't." I thought I heard bitterness in her voice. "You don't sound fond of Nellie."

"I wasn't."

"Why not?"

"Because she ruined the best man this town ever raised."

"Your man?"

She shook her head. She wouldn't answer.

I studied Thelma. She had her comforter back. But she didn't look any happier than she had earlier this morning. And the walnuts she was hulling seemed more a reason to keep her hands busy than anything else. It seemed everyone in Oakalla had changed since I found the Cadillac. Or maybe I was just looking for it.

"Does a 1936 Cadillac convertible mean anything to you?" I asked.

"No. Why should it?"

"I just wondered."

I rose and stretched. Thelma wasn't very talkative, but I had another question. I might as well ask it.

"You wouldn't by chance have seen Wilmer Wiemer in the neighborhood last night, would you?"

She suddenly got busy hulling walnuts. "What if I did?"

"I just wondered what he was up to."

"Why don't you ask him? Better yet, ask his wife. She

seems to know all of Wilmer's business. Or thinks she does."

I pulled off my gloves and laid them on the porch. "I might just do that. Thanks, Thelma."

I didn't go home. Instead I walked to the Corner Bar and Grill, ate a barbecue sandwich and a piece of pumpkin pie a la mode, and drank a glass of milk. Milk two days in a row. I felt almost pious.

Wilmer Wiemer lived on West Jackson Street in a colonial brick house with white marble pillars and a second-floor balcony where many a dignitary had sat in years past watching Oakalla's Fourth of July parade. Once on the edge of town, it still had the flavor of country, though it was now well within the limits of Oakalla. And when the wind was fresh, sifting through the two giant blue spruce that shaded the front lawn, it made you stop and drink your fill and wish you had five more minutes to spare.

I wondered where Wilmer's wife was. If she wasn't at work, she should be outside raking leaves on a day like this, if only to rake them from one pile to another and back again. I tried to remember if I'd ever seen her. I didn't think so. Not recently anyway.

I climbed the steps and knocked on the white wooden door. I could hear footsteps inside, but it seemed a long time before the door opened. "Yes, what is it?" The woman who asked had the frail whiney look of an invalid. Her skin was an off-white, almost transparent, and there was no spark in her pale green eyes.

"Mrs. Wiemer?" I asked.

"Yes. Who are you?"

"Garth Ryland. I'm editor of the *Oakalla Reporter*."

"Yes, I've read your paper." And from the tone of her voice probably used it to wrap her garbage.

But she opened the door wide enough for me to step inside. I hesitated. It was awfully cool and dark in there,

74

not unlike the Brainard mansion, and I had an unhealthy fear of bats. "Mr. Ryland?"

"Coming." I followed her down a dim hall, wondering what I'd got myself into now. Finally we made a sharp left and I stopped dead in my tracks. I'd entered the brightest, most spacious room I'd seen lately. Maybe twenty by twenty, it had at least a ten-foot ceiling and was constructed so that no corner went unlit. Hanging here and there from the hand-hewn walnut beams were green plants of every size and description.

"Well, what do you think?" she asked.

I was staring at a monstrous hanging fern. You could get lost in there and not come out for a week. "I like it," I said. "I like it a lot. But how do you do it without windows?"

"It's done by fluorescent lighting that substitutes for sunlight. My father installed it many years ago when he built this room."

"Your father was an architect?"

"No, my father was a hatter, among other things. He built it for me when he learned my skin was poisoned by direct sunlight. It's my very favorite of all my rooms."

She did look better in here, younger and more alive. With her red hair and green eyes I imagined she was quite the leprechaun in her younger days. Her wedding pictures on the mantle above the fireplace seemed to confirm that impression, and even Wilmer, in his black tuxedo and bow tie, looked more dapper than dandy. I wondered what had happened to her and Wilmer. They didn't look as happy today as then.

"You still haven't told me what you're doing here," she gently reminded me. "Not that I mind your company. . . . It's rare I have any. But there *are* things I could be doing."

I looked around. It seemed all the things here had already been done long ago. "How well do you know your husband, Mrs. Wiemer?"

75

"Well enough to anticipate that question and at the same time not answer it."

"You know he's been trying to buy Paul Black's farm for years?"

"I'm aware of that. Yes."

"I just wondered if you knew why."

"No. I don't know why. Wilmer keeps his own counsel. And frankly, that's the way I prefer it."

"You don't approve of his wheeling and dealing?"

"I neither approve, nor disapprove. It just doesn't interest me, that's all." Neither did my line of questioning. I was fast wearing out my welcome. "But if you object, why don't you use your paper to mobilize the citizens of Oakalla against him? You can write very persuasively when you choose to, though I can't say you choose to all of the time."

"I'm not out to get Wilmer. Not unless he steps on my toes."

"Then what are you after?"

I studied her. Color had crept into her face. Perhaps even anticipation. If I was after her, now was as good a time as any to ask. I bit my tongue. For a long moment I considered it.

"The truth," I said weakly.

She fielded it expertly and threw it back to me. "The truth to what? The truth itself is rather large."

"To where Wilmer went last night and why."

"He went nowhere last night. He was home in bed."

"You're sure?"

"We . . . we have separate bedrooms. But I can assure you I know when my husband is home or not."

She was either lying or it wasn't Wilmer I saw last night. Whatever the case, I'd said the wrong thing. But now that I had my foot in my mouth and the lady upset, how did I make my exit? Give her a straight arm and run for the door? "I'm sorry, Mrs. Wiemer. I was sure I saw him there."

"Saw him where?"

"The old Brainard estate." Not exactly true, but at least he was in the neighborhood.

"If you're as sorry as you want me to believe, perhaps you'll answer a question for me. What were *you* doing out there last night?"

"Hunting nightcrawlers. They're over a dollar a dozen now."

She brightened. "Really?" She took my arm and led the way to the front door. "Then perhaps you'd like to stop by here tonight? I hear the worm hunting can be quite good."

"Which yard, front or back?"

"The back. In fact, it's best right under Wilmer's bedroom window." She opened the door to let me out. "But remember, Mr. Ryland, if nominated, I won't run; if elected, I won't serve. If you have an ax to grind with Wilmer, don't ask me to turn the wheel. I've helped you all I will."

"Why?" I had to ask. "Why tell me this much?"

"Have you ever played the fool?" she asked.

"Who hasn't?"

"Did you like it much?"

"No, not much."

She smiled sadly just before she closed the door. "Neither do I."

From there I went door to door, gathering opinions about marijuana. As yesterday, everyone had an opinion. No one had seen Woody. I began to wonder if I weren't looking in the wrong direction.

9

At home Ruth had supper ready to put on the table—swiss steak, browned potatoes, fresh frozen corn, and persimmon pudding for dessert.

"No, Diana didn't call," was the first thing she said to me.

"It's been a month," I answered.

"One you've survived."

"I guess I have at that."

I gave Ruth a smile. Though her scowl was withering as usual, she seemed genuinely glad to see me. And on time for once. Beneath that brassy exterior was a caring friend. Often impatient. Quick to judge and slow to forgive. Not always on my terms, but always on my side.

And since Diana had left, the only woman in my life. That meant a lot to me. For without a woman to balance me, I tended to flop around, like a kite without a tail, making a lot of waves, but not getting anywhere. Men and women needed each other—as friends, if not as lovers. Not necessarily to make life less lonely, though it helped, but to make it rounder, less cutting at the edges, and more in the shape of the earth.

Ruth handed me a platter of Swiss steak, retrieving a mushroom that had fallen on the table. "Eat up," she said, "before it gets cold."

I ate up, then had a second helping. But I still left room for persimmon pudding.

"Something bothering you?" she asked. "You've hardly touched your supper."

I smiled at her. "A lot of things."

She got up and poured me a cup of coffee. "Care to elaborate?"

"You knew Woody Padgett was missing?"

"I've heard. Why is that any concern of yours?"

"The fact he's making something for me. Besides, I like Woody."

"So do I, such as he is."

"How's that?"

"Two bricks short of a load."

"A lot of people are. You can't hold that against him," I said.

"I don't. But then when he's gone for a night, I don't spend the next day looking for him, like you did."

"Who told you that?"

"Word gets around."

"Rupert is busy looking for marijuana. I decided to give him a hand."

"And when did he deputize you?"

She was zeroing in on me. Before long she'd put it all together and come up with the Cadillac. I didn't want that to happen. "Do you mind if we change the subject?"

"Fine. What do you want to talk about?"

"Nellie Brainard," I said.

"What about her?"

"Where did she come from, for one thing?" I'd heard Nellie was an orphan.

"Some say she got kicked out of hell. But that might be too harsh. How do you know Nellie Brainard? I thought she was before your time."

Almost before my time. Once, along about dusk, when I was riding my bicycle past the Brainard mansion, I saw Nellie standing at the end of the lane. Stock-still. Staring at something with narrow-eyed intent, the way a cat stares at a mouse.

I tried to explain Nellie's look to Grandmother Ryland, but lacked the wherewithal to put it into words. Grandmother just laughed at me. She said I had nothing to fear from Nellie, that if I'd leave Nellie's apples alone, she would leave me alone.

I wanted to believe her, but only partially succeeded. It seemed from that day on, whenever I rode my bicycle past the Brainard mansion, I edged a little farther forward on the seat and the pedals turned a little faster.

"I remember her," I said. "She was one of the ghosts of my childhood."

"You weren't alone. She was everybody's ghost here in Oakalla."

"Tell me more."

"Why?"

"It sounds like a good story. You know how I like a good story."

She gave me a knowing look. She didn't know what my game was, but she was on to me. "What's it worth to you?"

"I'll do supper dishes tonight."

"You do supper dishes every night you're here."

"I'll even dry them and put them away."

"I'll settle for that."

She got up and brought me my persimmon pudding. "Here. This might take a while."

As she poured herself another cup of coffee, I

reached for the whipped cream and plopped a spoonful on top of my pudding. If I was going to be decadent, I planned to get my money's worth.

"Nellie was an orphan," she began. "She came here when she was about twelve. The Metzgers took her in. Old Marvin and Eunice. They never had any kids of their own and they were looking for someone to pour on—all that dusty love and money they'd been hoarding over the years. They took Nellie into their hearts, small though they were, and gave her anything she wanted. Which, considering Nellie's appetite, was considerable. They asked God for a little breeze to freshen their lives. He sent them a full-blown tornado. Once headed, she couldn't be stopped. But to their credit Marvin and Eunice tried. Eunice more than Marvin maybe. When Nellie was about sixteen, they tried to tighten the reins on her. But by then it was way too late. Things went from bad to worse until Nellie was the next thing to a prisoner in her own home. She'd run off; the sheriff would bring her back, and then Eunice would take a razor strap to her and ground her for another month. It would've been best for all concerned if they'd just let Nellie go her own way. But they were determined to make a lady out of her if it killed them. Which it nearly did. Nellie picked up a meat fork one night and started after Eunice. She aimed to put it in Eunice's eye, but missed and struck her in the forehead instead. Nearly blinded her the way it was. After that Marvin and Eunice weren't long in shipping her out of town. No one knew where for sure. Some said a boarding school down South. Others said she never made it that far. In any case Nellie stayed gone for nearly a year."

"Why did she come back?"

"Marvin and Eunice drove off the road and killed themselves. At least that's the way it looked. Nellie showed up on their doorstep a few days later looking for her inheritance."

"Did she get it?"

"Nope. Marvin and Eunice left every last penny to the Fair Haven Church. All Nellie got was the family Bible."

"Then she married Big-Ears Brainard?" I asked.

"A couple months later, long enough for her to get her hooks into him. Or his into her. He always did like them young, if you know what I mean."

I knew what she meant. "Then he wasn't exactly a harmless old poop drifting through life, waiting to be plucked by the likes of Nellie?"

"No. She met her match there. All she saw of his money was what she needed for groceries. And precious little of that."

"Then he did have money?"

"Rumor said he did. Though by the way he lived no one could ever prove it. To make matters worse for Nellie, he wouldn't let her out of his sight. He drove her everywhere she went."

"Which wasn't very far or very often."

"You're catching on. She'd gone from the frying pan into the fire."

"Then Big-Ears drove away one day and never came back. At least as far as we know," I said.

"Right again."

"Why would he do that?"

"Maybe he finally realized he had a wildcat by the tail."

"Why not just divorce her?"

"Divorce costs money. Or don't you know that?"

I nodded. I knew that.

"Why would he leave and not take his money with him?"

"He wouldn't. Not unless he was planning to come back for it."

"Which brings me to my next question," I said. "Do you think he ever came back?"

82

"In what form?"

"Alive. The only form I know."

"Rumor has it he did. He came back and stayed."

"I don't see how he could have."

"You asked. I told you," she said. "I don't believe it any more than you do, but an awful lot of people around here swear they've heard him working on the place. Too many for all of them to be hearing things."

"But no one's ever seen him?"

"No. Not that I know of. But between you and me something's going on out there. Otherwise, the place would've fallen down years ago. Especially with all the traffic it had."

"What traffic is that?"

"The people looking for Big-Ears' money. They figured Nellie never found it and Big-Ears forgot where it was—or he wouldn't have been out there digging for it."

"Big-Ears was *seen* digging for it?"

"No. But a lot of holes turned up that people couldn't explain."

"Couldn't they have been made by someone in town?"

"They could have. But people here tend to look out for their own. If somebody here was making them, somebody else here would know about it."

That made sense. At least the first part did. People in Oakalla, as in most small towns, did tend to look out for their own. "When was this, do you remember?"

"After Nellie left. Maybe within a year or so. Not many had the courage to go on the place while she was still here."

"And she left without a trace?"

"As far as I know. But then I haven't been looking for her."

"Do you think she's still alive?"

"Your guess is as good as mine. Do you want her to be?"

"I'm not sure what I want at this point. Do me a favor, will you, Ruth. See what you can find out about a big bald man with small red ears. I'd guess he's somewhere around sixty. He looks something like a walrus and drives a black Mercedes, if that helps any."

"Do you have a name?"

"He didn't give me one."

"That's not much to go on."

"No, it isn't. But then you don't need much."

She smiled at that. "Any particular reason why you're interested in him?"

"I met him today out at the Brainard mansion. He said he owned the place. I'd like to know how."

"What were you doing out at the Brainard mansion?"

"Looking for Woody."

"What would he be doing out there?"

"Nothing that I know of. I'd just run out of other places to look."

"What about Wilmer Wiemer?" she asked.

"What about him?"

"Do you still want me to find out why he's interested in Paul Black's farm?"

"More than ever."

"Which comes first, the walrus or Wilmer?"

"I'll take either one. Whichever's easier."

"I'll start with the walrus. I'll put Aunt Emma to work on Wilmer. She never did have much use for him anyway. Of course, you could say that for most of Oakalla. Though not many let on."

"I met his wife today," I said. "It must be lonely being Wilmer."

"It must be lonely being Wilmer's wife," she answered. "At least he's out and among the living."

"Lonely for everyone concerned," I agreed.

A couple of hours later I left by the back door, circled the house, and started uptown with the faint hope that

Ruth wouldn't notice I was gone. It was a beautiful night, cool and still, the white hunter's moon ringed by a faint corona in an otherwise cloudless sky.

I went to Wilmer Wiemer's house and hid in the shadows in Wilmer's backyard. I'd been there about a half hour, just long enough to get thoroughly chilled, when I heard something scrape the side of the house. Then Wilmer appeared. Holding onto a rope tied to something inside his bedroom, he walked down the bricks and landed softly in the yard. Though he didn't seem to be in a hurry, once he got underway I had to run to keep up with him.

He headed east, then north, keeping to the shadows and stopping every hundred yards to look around, like a fox on the prowl. Could this be the same Wilmer I knew—the one who drove a Lincoln Continental, the one who sat stolidly behind his desk counting his assets like an incarnation of Ebeneezer Scrooge, the one who held the mortgages of half of Oakalla? He reminded me of a kid sneaking out on his parents. Where he was going didn't seem nearly as important as getting there and back.

We were on Fair Haven Road approaching the city limits. For a moment I thought he was headed for the Brainard mansion. Then he made a quick right and disappeared into a shadow. I waited for him to come out again, and when he didn't, I went to investigate.

He was standing in front of Edgar's shop, trying to raise the overhead door. When he couldn't, he went around to the side door and tried it. It, too, was locked.

He pulled a ring of keys from his pocket and tried each one in turn. He got lucky on about the sixth try, as the lock tripped and the door opened. But before he could get inside, the porch light came on and Edgar stepped outside holding a shotgun. Wilmer ducked around the corner of the shop just in time, while I stayed frozen to the shadow I was in.

Edgar walked to the shop, found the door open, and

went inside. When the shop light came on, I moved. I didn't want to have to explain to Edgar what I was doing there. Or what Wilmer was doing there. I'd give Wilmer a chance later.

I stopped beside a utility pole long enough to get my breath. I'd gone north, not south, and now had to figure out a way to get back into town without being seen. Then something caught my eye and made me wish I'd gone the other way. The moonlight was glinting off something shiny near the Brainard mansion. From where I stood, it looked like the chrome of a car.

A quarter mile later I stopped at Nellie Brainard's lane. If there was a car parked behind the mansion, I couldn't see it from here. I'd have to get closer.

Part of me said to go on. What could be finer than a midnight stroll through an acre of briers and cockleburs? The other part of me, the part that was the brighter of the two, said enough was enough, that I'd been pressing my luck lately and never had much to begin with. I should have listened to it.

I hadn't gone three steps down the lane when I realized I wasn't alone in there. Something a few yards ahead of me was being very careful to move when I did. Using an old pheasant hunting tactic, I stopped and counted to ten, hoping that whoever was out there would get nervous in the silence and flush. When it didn't, I began to walk slowly in a zigzag course to make sure it didn't double back on me. All my old hunting instincts returned with a rush, and I could almost feel the Stevens in my hands, as my eyes narrowed and my trigger finger began to itch.

The stalk went on for several minutes. Every time I thought my quarry had got behind me, I'd double back and come again. I was approaching the end of the lane, and there was nothing ahead but fifty feet of bare yard before the mansion. Still, I'd seen nothing so far, heard

86

only the whisper of dried grass as if I were chasing a spectre. It was unnerving. Here I was, the great white hunter all poised for a shot, and I didn't even have a popgun. What if I were stalking a cape buffalo instead of a field mouse? It'd be my head they'd be mounting on the wall.

Wham! I never heard a thing. Someone sprang up from somewhere behind me and hit me with what felt like the trunk of a tree. Fortunately for me it was half rotten or it would have put more than my lights out.

A few minutes later I got up and wobbled into the yard of the Brainard mansion where I sat for several more minutes. The moon seemed to have suddenly brightened, and every time I opened my eyes to look, a bomb went off in my brain. I finally found the courage to touch my hand to the back of my head. Reassuring. It was there after all. Even better, none of my brains had leaked out. I needed every ounce I had, and sometimes, like tonight, even that fell far short.

Finally I got up and walked around to the back of the mansion. The car, if that's what it had been, was gone, leaving a trail of torn brambles all the way to the road. I looked at the Brainard mansion, as dark and imposing as ever, thought for a split second about going in there, and decided against it. It didn't look even half good in daylight. It wouldn't look any better at night. Besides, I didn't have a flashlight, nor did I know who might be waiting for me in there. Whoever it was, I wasn't particularly eager to find out.

Then a sickening feeling overtook me. It was partly from the lump on my head but mostly from worry about the Cadillac. In my haste to find out who was here, I'd left it unprotected. It could be ashes by now.

I began to limp up the lane, following what I thought by now was a car path. I was making good time despite the three pounds of cockleburs I was wearing around each ankle. Then prudence and a jolt that left me rubber-legged told me to slow down, that if the Cadillac was marked for destruction, it was already too late to save it. It wasn't. It still sat safely inside the shop. Edgar sat beside it, still holding his shotgun. With my hands up I went in to join him.

10

I sat staring at the breakfast table. I yawned. My back ached; my head still hurt, and the bags under my eyes felt like water balloons. If I didn't get my act together soon, I wouldn't need a costume for Halloween.

Ruth seemed almost birdlike by comparison. I'd never seen her look quite so chipper in the morning, or maybe I was so far down a corpse would've seemed lively by comparison.

"I see you've been burning the candle at both ends again," she said, pouring me a second cup of coffee. "You're getting too old for that."

"Tell me something I don't already know." I felt the knot on the back of my head and winced.

Ruth didn't miss a trick. Within seconds, on the pretense of clearing the table, she was right behind me, staring a hole in my neck. "Care to tell me about it?" she asked.

"About what?"

She not so gently tapped the knot on my head, as I ducked away. "About that."

"I got hit by a falling star."

"Lucky it didn't hit anything vital."

I couldn't argue with that.

The phone rang. Ruth answered it, then pointed at me. "Who is it?" I asked. I didn't want to move unless I had to.

"Edgar."

I felt my stomach turn over. "Tell him I'm not here."

"He said to tell you he's not here," she repeated to Edgar. Then she turned back to me. "He says to get over there right away."

"Why?" I asked.

"Why?" she repeated. Then back to me. "Never mind. Just get over there."

"I'm on my way," I said.

She didn't bother to repeat that. She just hung up.

Edgar was waiting for me outside his shop. I was sure he was going to tell me to find another home for the Cadillac. He was leaning that way last night, but said he'd sleep on it.

Instead he said, "Be here first thing tomorrow."

"Why?"

"We're going to restore the Cadillac. The sooner it's out of my hair, the easier I'll breathe."

"Couldn't you have told me that over the phone?"

"I could have. But seeing how you've put me out lately, I figured I owed you one."

"Thanks, Edgar. You're all heart."

I started walking home. Two blocks later Rupert picked me up. "What's new with you?" he asked, putting the car in gear and driving slowly down my street.

"I got hit over the head last night. What's new with you?"

"I found a report I've been missing for three weeks. I'd filed it under the wrong letter."

"But no marijuana?"

"No marijuana. Now the pilot's missing. He's not been seen since Monday."

"Maybe somebody got to him," I said.

"Maybe they did." He didn't even glance my way. "Where did you get hit in the head?"

"The back. Right behind my left ear."

"Where else?"

"The Brainard estate."

"What were you doing out there?"

"I started out following Wilmer Wiemer. But I lost him and ended up there."

"Is Wilmer the one who hit you?"

"I'm not sure. Wilmer or whoever was driving the car I saw parked there."

"There were two of them there?"

"I think so. I was following one. The other was waiting for me."

"Did you get a good look at the car?"

"No. But I'd look for one with a lot of scratches on it." I pulled up my pants leg to show him. "They'll look a lot like these."

"I'll keep that in mind. Any idea what it was doing there?"

"No."

He pulled out his tobacco pouch to take a chew, then changed his mind. "You think it has anything to do with the Cadillac?"

"What Cadillac?"

"Your Cadillac. The one you've got hidden away in Edgar's shop. The one that almost burned up Tuesday night, though neither you nor Edgar bothered to report it."

"Oh, that Cadillac."

"I'm serious, Garth. It's awful hard to milk a cow while you're riding her."

"Meaning?"

"Just that. I know you want to find Woody, but for some reason you want to keep that Cadillac out of it. Someday you might have to decide which is more important to you."

"So what do you want to know about the Cadillac?" I asked.

"Who it belongs to, for starters. Where you found it. Where it's going to next."

"It belongs to me. I found it in a barn. And it's going to Ruth for her birthday as soon as it's restored. You're free to impound it any time you want to. Anything else?"

He stopped the car in front of my house. "Get some sleep. You need it."

A shave and a shower later I drove to my newspaper office and spent the next several hours organizing the interviews I'd had and getting the *Oakalla Reporter* ready to print. Since Sniffy Smith was the first one I'd interviewed, I gave him top billing. That should get everyone's attention.

I wondered whether I should report Woody's disappearance and decided against it. For one thing I didn't know how far gone he was. If he was alive and well and out on a lark, nothing would be served by reporting him missing—except to draw attention to him and me and perhaps the Cadillac. If he was dead, nothing would be served by it either, except to alert whoever had killed him. When in doubt I fell back on the old saying, "It's better to remain silent and be thought a fool, than to open your mouth and remove all doubt."

It was late afternoon when I finally finished and drove to the Brainard mansion. I took Jessie to the first bramble bush and left her there. Any farther down the lane, and she'd think of some way to get even.

I started walking toward the mansion. It was quiet out here today, unusually quiet. No birds singing, no tractors humming, no pigs squealing, no leaves turning. Just the scurry of locusts at my feet. And as the sun dipped behind the oaks with the first cool lick of evening, I felt like the last man on earth.

I quietly entered the mansion, went through the dining room, and started up the rosewood stairs. It was slow going. There was something oppressive about this place that settled in my legs and made them hard to lift. I told myself I was just tired, that all I needed was a good night's sleep. But I couldn't escape the feeling that if I poked around in here long enough, something large and ugly was going to come crawling out at me.

I searched the upstairs, stopping in Nellie's bedroom. Her huge bed loomed even larger today than I remembered it; its carved savage faces were even more hideous. Even Nellie looked somehow sinister. As beautiful as ever, but deadly as well. There was something in her eyes that hinted of madness. But there was something else even more frightening, the something I'd glimpsed along Fair Haven Road as a boy. It was a brightly focused intelligence, one that burned with a white heat and was capable of everything and anything. I understood now why Nellie's foster parents were no match for her. It would have taken Prometheus himself to steal her fire. And then at the risk of his life.

I went downstairs and into the kitchen. The checkered linoleum was warped and chipped where the stove sat, and there were grease spots on the walls and the smell of grease imbedded in the linoleum itself. Strange. The stove was here. So was the refrigerator. So was Nellie's bed upstairs. It almost seemed that she expected to come back.

I went into the pantry. There on the floor I found a bread wrapper and part of a jug of milk that was just starting to sour. It couldn't have been there more than a couple days.

I heard something fall in the basement. It sounded like it was right under me. A couple minutes later I heard something else fall. A possum? I wondered. I had one in my basement once. It sounded like the Seventh Army was holding maneuvers down there. Even Ruth wouldn't go down to face it, and she'd face about anything. But somehow I doubted this was a possum.

I sat tight for several minutes, as the noise in the basement continued. Whoever it was, he or she would never make it as a cat burglar. Then I heard someone coming up the basement stairs. I opened the pantry door a crack, just enough to see out. With each footfall on the stairs I felt my heart beat a little faster. I wondered if spying would be considered an aerobic exercise.

Thelma Osterday burst through the basement door and into the kitchen. Her hands were doubled into fists. She looked like she planned to kill whoever it was she was looking for. I hoped it wasn't me.

I didn't know what to do. If I yelled at her, the shock might kill one or both of us. If I didn't, the moment would be lost. Once back on her home ground, Thelma would be a lot tougher nut to crack.

I decided to risk it. I opened the pantry door and spoke just as calmly as I could. "Thelma?"

She wheeled and faced me. For a very long moment I thought she was going to charge. "Garth Ryland! You just gave me the scare of my life!"

"Well, don't feel like the Lone Ranger. It took me about twenty years to wait for you to walk up those stairs."

Her shock passed. Anger replaced it. "What are you doing here spying on me?" she asked.

"I'm not spying on you. I didn't even know you were here. Not until I heard you in the basement."

"Then what are you doing here in the first place?"

"I might ask you the same thing."

"You first. You're farther away from home than I am," she said.

94

"I'm looking for Woody Padgett," I answered. "You haven't by any chance seen him, have you?"

Her eyes said she hadn't. But something in her face said she had. Or wished she had. I couldn't tell which. "No. I haven't seen him."

"Since when?"

"Since Monday."

That was news to me. "When Monday?"

"You didn't let me finish," she said. "It was Monday a week ago. Woody stopped by to bring me those walnuts I was hulling yesterday."

I studied her. I couldn't tell if she was telling the truth or not. "Why would Woody take the trouble to bring you walnuts?"

"Woody and I go way back. About as far back as two people can go."

"You grew up together?"

"Two doors apart. I'm ten months older than he is."

She seemed more than ten months older than Woody. Maybe because he seemed so young. "You never told me that before," I said.

"The subject of Woody never came up before." Her face softened. So did her voice. Then she smiled at me. For a moment Thelma and I were on the same wavelength. It was like old times again. The moment passed.

"Your turn," I said.

"My turn to do what?"

"Tell me what you're doing here."

"Why is that any business of yours?"

"I thought we had an agreement."

"We did. You went first. I didn't say anything about going second. Good-bye, Garth. It was nice talking to you." She opened the back door.

"What are you hiding, Thelma?"

The arrow struck home. It stopped her in her tracks. "I'm not hiding anything." But she wouldn't look at me.

"I think you are. You haven't been yourself the past couple of days. You're worried about something. It shows all over your face."

"If I am, that's my business."

"Maybe so. But if you tell me what it is, I might be able to help."

"The best way to help is to go on about your business and leave me to mine. What I know can't help either one of us."

"Help us do what?"

She didn't answer. She closed the door and left.

I left by the front door. It wasn't until I reached Jessie that I stopped to look back. The sun had just slipped below the horizon, draping a shadow across the face of the mansion, making it more forbidding than ever. Nothing to fear from it. Not really. Buildings couldn't hurt you. Only the people in them. But I very much doubted I'd ever grow to like the place.

I left Jessie at home and walked to the Corner Bar and Grill. Tonight was Ruth's bowling night, and I didn't feel like staying home alone. I wanted company—lots of it.

I had a beer, then another after that one went down so well. The Corner began to fill up, as the regulars came in with their friends and families and whoever else happened to be on the street at the time. I didn't mind at all. As far as I was concerned, the more the merrier. Maybe they weren't the world's elite, maybe they drank beer and played euchre and ate catfish and onion rings, maybe they drove pickups and liked football and talked weather, but they wore easily, like a pair of old moccasins, and were my kind of people.

I noticed Wilmer Wiemer sitting at the other end of the bar. The stools on each side of him were vacant, so I took one of them. I could tell by the glaze in his eyes that he'd been here longer than I had. He smiled when he saw me and raised his glass. Together we drank to Thursday night blues.

96

"You know, Garth, old buddy," he said, "you're all right. You don't like me and you don't pretend you do. But at least you're up front about it, not like the rest of this chickenshit town." Wilmer took another drink, then continued his soliloquy. "Yes, sir. Old Wilmer gets a lot of smiles, but when it comes right down to it, he ain't loved. He ain't even liked very well. Hell, half the people in here wouldn't spit in my eye to put a fire out. The other half would. You can't win. No matter how you slice the cake, somebody always gets the biggest piece. Is that my fault?" He pounded the bar with his fists. "Is that my fault, Garth?"

"No, it's not your fault."

"Hell no, it ain't my fault! I was as poor as any son-of-a-bitch in here and look where I am now! I own this town! Half of it anyway."

I looked around. Wilmer was starting to attract attention, and like any loud drunk, he was starting to ruin everybody else's good time.

He waved the bartender over to us. "Tell me straight, Hiram, what you really think about me. You think I'm a pimp, don't you? An undergrown, windblown dried up piece of shit?"

Hiram nearly swallowed his snuff before he could answer. "Hell, Wilmer, I don't think about you one way or another."

Wilmer rocked back on his stool, then rocked forward, almost landing on the bar. "Imagine that! He don't think about me one way or another," he mimicked. Hiram meanwhile was gliding down the bar away from us as fast as he could go. But not fast enough. "Where you going?" Wilmer yelled. "I want another round. For me and my old buddy Garth here."

"No more for me, Hiram. Thanks," I said.

"Come on, Garth, the night's still young," Wilmer insisted. "And this is my night to howl!" To prove it he let out a howl that even killed the jukebox. I looked for somewhere to hide, but there wasn't room under my stool. Wilmer was already there. "What happened?" he asked as I helped him up. "When I went to flush it, I couldn't find the handle."

"Wilmer, would you consider a drive somewhere?" I asked.

"Oh, hell no, I can't even walk."

"I mean if I drive your car?"

He downed the last of his Jack Daniels as he considered it. "You promise not to take me home? I don't think I can stand to be there one more night. I might break down the door to her bedroom."

"Maybe it's time you did."

"Hell, if I thought it'd do any good, I'd have done it a long time ago. It only works in the movies. Not where I live." He found his cowboy hat and put it on, then tipped it to all the women on his way out. "Queens, they all look like queens tonight."

I drove the Lincoln for over an hour, as Wilmer sat beside me blissfully crocked and totally unrestrained, like a kid on his first bender. He told me things he'd probably never told anyone before, would never tell anyone again, and which in more polite company he'd deny to his dying day.

We were southwest of Oakalla, heading back to town, when I noticed a car ahead of us. It rounded a curve, then cut its lights and disappeared. I didn't think anything about it until I realized we were at the western edge of Paul Black's farm and that to the east on the next rise I could see the silhouette of Woody's barn.

"You mind if we stop a minute, Wilmer?"

He sat up straight and looked around. "What for?"

"The car ahead of us just turned off its lights. I want to see where it's going."

"Why?"

98

"You know me, Wilmer, your old buddy, Garth. I like to know what's going on."

"Is that why you came by my house the other day, started asking my wife a bunch of questions?"

"Who told you that?"

"She did. She also told me she didn't give you any answers."

I couldn't gauge Wilmer's mood. He seemed hurt, going on surly. "I was just doing my job," I said.

"Which is what, sticking your nose in other people's business?"

"Woody is missing. I wondered why."

"And you think I have something to do with it? Why in the hell would I want to trouble Possum? He has nothing I want."

"Possum?" I interrupted.

"Woody."

"How did he get the name Possum?"

"I gave it to him. For playing possum. He was good at it, the best I ever saw. He could flat out make you believe he was dead, even when you knew he wasn't."

"That good, huh?" This was starting to get interesting.

"I'll tell you how good. One time when we were climbing a tree, he fell out and landed hard. Then he just laid there and wouldn't move, no matter what I said. I'll fix you, I thought. So I climbed down from the tree and began twisting his ears. When that didn't work, I honked his nose. I even dragged him around the tree by his hair. Then I got scared and went for help. When I came back, he was up in the tree laughing at me."

"I didn't know Woody had it in him."

"There's a lot of things about Possum you don't know."

"Such as?"

He never got a chance to answer. I saw a light in

Woody's house go on. Wilmer saw it, too, and understood immediately. He was out of the car before I was.

We didn't need a light. Though on the wane the moon was bright enough to see by. Not clearly. Not bright enough to see the fine print on the NO TRESPASSING sign, but bright enough to see Wilmer's head bobbing like a silver apple, as he led me on a zigzag course through the trees. It seemed, by the route he took, that he knew his way around these woods a lot better than I did. He'd been here before.

We came to Stony Creek. There was a breeze overhead, sawing the limbs back and forth in creaks and groans, but the valley floor was unruffled. Stony Creek was ribbon smooth as it slid along like the bright steel of a knife.

I heard a coon or possum shuffling through the leaves ahead of us. I saw a nighthawk dip and float by on its way upstream. I smelled the wild sweet scent of the autumn woods, the faint scent of burning cedar, and felt the tug of autumns past. I was aware, alert, alive—enjoying myself more than I wanted to admit.

Following him, I realized that Wilmer felt the same way. It wasn't the prize he wanted nearly as much as the chase. We were like two boys playing hooky from school. We were too immersed in doing it to think about the consequences.

We started up the hill toward Woody's barn. By now the weight of the drinks had begun to take their toll on Wilmer, and his step became more a plod than a prance. We rested at the top of the hill, as Wilmer caught his breath. Then the light in Woody's house went out.

I put my finger to my lips for silence, then pointed to the house. I could have saved the effort. The moment after I did, I heard Woody's pickup start up. It was already on its way down the drive when we reached the barnyard and going too fast for us to ever catch up to it.

The pickup turned west on Creek Road. A moment later I heard a car pull onto Creek Road from the dead end road and follow the pickup west. Wilmer's Lincoln was at least a quarter of a mile away. We didn't have a chance to catch them. We didn't even try.

"What do you think?" I asked Wilmer.

"It could be kids. A lot of them park around here. I know I used to."

"What would kids be doing up here?"

"Snooping around. Kids are always someplace they ain't supposed to be. A missing man's house would be a natural attraction."

"I don't think it was kids," I said.

"Who was it then?"

"Maybe it was Woody."

He gave me a strange look that might have meant anything and said, "And maybe that's something you don't want to know."

"Says who?" I asked.

"Says me."

"What aren't you telling me, Wilmer?"

"Whatever it is, it's for your own good."

We went inside Woody's house. Nothing was missing as far as we could tell. And except for a few shuffled papers, there was no real evidence that anyone else had been there. We turned off the light and closed the door on our way out.

"Do you know where this road leads?" I asked Wilmer, as we walked toward the Lincoln.

"Which fork, north or south?"

"The south fork."

"Nowhere in particular. Some call it the Colburn Road, but, hell, you have to make ten turns between here and Colburn. You might as well call it the Woodhollow Road. It's off in that direction too. Or the Madison Road, if you want to stretch it far enough."

"Woodhollow Sanitarium?" I asked.

"Right. It's been there for years, as long as I can remember anyway." And by the tone of his voice, longer than he wanted to remember.

We climbed into the Lincoln and drove toward town. Wilmer seemed especially attentive, noting every detail of the landscape, like a man on his way to the gallows. Finally he said, "Take me home."

"I thought you didn't want to go home."

"I don't. But sometimes there's no place else to go."

I left Wilmer and the Lincoln off at his house and walked to the *Oakalla Reporter*. The first thing I did when I got there was to try to call Rupert. He wasn't home. His wife, Elvira, said he was still on duty. She didn't come right out and say it but hinted strongly that I might find him somewhere outside the missing pilot's house. That meant Rupert was still knee-deep in the marijuana hunt. Not much help there.

I hung up the receiver, then picked it up again. I dialed one, and six more numbers before I stopped. The second time I dialled all eight numbers. Diana's line was busy. I wondered who was on the other end, whom she'd be talking to at this late hour. Not me. I could vouch for that. Better I didn't think about it.

I went to work and four hours later put that week's edition of the *Oakalla Reporter* to bed. Reading it over one last time before giving it to my printer, I was pleased with what I'd done. Not a great effort, but my best in several weeks, and one that I hoped would spark some local interest because I'd ended my column, "This is what your neighbors think about marijuana. Now let us hear what you think." If that didn't get a response, nothing would.

I didn't go home. Instead I walked to Edgar's shop and looked in on the Cadillac. It appeared to be resting quietly. Then I took a seat beside the shop. The night was skittish, the wind uncertain about its direction. So were my thoughts. There were a lot of possibilities, but all I knew for certain was that Woody was missing, and I shared part of the blame. So apparently did the Cadillac. But the whys and wherefores eluded me. I thought perhaps that once the Cadillac was restored and safely in Ruth's hands, its debts, whatever they were, would be canceled; peace would reign again, and Woody would return safely home. I was wrong as usual.

11

It took us nearly a week, working night and day, to restore the Cadillac and get it running again. During that entire time I wore a permanent five o'clock shadow and enough dirt to grow tulips. We had to replace all the hoses and all the belts, fix the radiator, tune the engine, and change the oil. And that was for starters.

While Edgar worked on the interior of the car, removing the rust and filling the holes, I had the dubious honor of putting the outside in order. I never did like sand, even as a boy, and I liked sanding even less. It didn't help that I had an electrical sander. Nor did it help that in this one particular area, the one he elected me to do, Edgar insisted on perfection. And every time I thought I finally had it right, he assured me I didn't.

"Whose car *is* this anyway?"

"Ruth's" was his stock answer.

"It seems we're going awfully slow."

"Garth, there are three things I never hurry. Making love, a good steak, and one of these old cars. What time put in it, it's going to take time to take out."

So I'd grin and bear it and go back to sanding until my nose and eyes were full of dust and my arms were ready to drop off. "Well?" I'd say, wanting his approval.

He'd crawl out of the Cadillac, squint his good eye, and say, "It needs a little more right here."

"You can't make a silk purse out of a sow's ear."

"But you can make a silk purse out of a silk purse. This is a thirty-six Cadillac you're talking about, not a Hobgoblin."

"I believe that's a *Gremlin*."

Then he'd shake his finger at me. "I don't care what it is. It still needs a little more right here."

So the week went until I became almost as particular as he. I knew I'd arrived when he nodded his approval and I said, "No. I think it needs a little more right here."

Then it was time to paint it. Edgar had his heart set on blue, but I told him that blue wasn't really Ruth's color. I wanted yellow, the original color, and he said that if she didn't like blue, she could hardly be expected to like yellow. We finally decided on gold, mainly because that's what Edgar had the most of.

And when we were finally finished, and the Cadillac sat there glowing in the dusk, making even Edgar's shop look brighter, I felt a satisfaction I hadn't felt in a long time. Usually I put my thoughts on paper for others to read. Then I had to wait for them to tell me I'd done a good job. Often praise came too seldom, and I was left to wonder just how good I was.

But today I didn't have to wonder. I knew what I'd done. I could see it with my own two eyes. It made me think of Woody, if perhaps he didn't have it right all along. You really didn't need a great mind when you had hands as wise as his. You really didn't need a great mind to do a lot of things useful and beautiful. Only a kind and gentle soul.

"What do you think?" Edgar asked, while walking around the Cadillac admiring his handiwork.

"I think we did a good job," I said.

He nodded in agreement, as he wiped a smudge of dirt off the paint. "It ain't perfect. It never is. But it's about as close as we could come to it."

Then he offered his hand; I shook it, and we sat down and each drank a cold beer to celebrate.

The next morning Ruth and I sat across the breakfast table from each other. She knew I was up to something. I'd gotten up first and put the coffee on.

"So where are you headed today?" she asked.

"I thought we'd take a drive in the country."

"Where to?"

"Here and there. I'll let you decide."

She gave me a sharp look. "Okay, what's up?"

"I don't know what you mean."

"What I mean is when was the last time we took a drive in the country?"

"It was as early as last year."

"More like two years ago Easter." She brightened. "You didn't by chance trade in that junk-heap of yours on a new car, did you? God forbid! It's too much to hope."

"Close. You're close, Ruth. Just wait here until I get back."

I left her buttering her toast and walked to Edgar's to pick up the Cadillac. Gassed and oiled and all ready to go, it sat waiting for me inside his shop. Chewing on a cigar and looking like the proud father, Edgar sat waiting for me too. He even opened the door for me and wiped off his fingerprints after I'd climbed inside.

"Just remember to take it easy," he said. "I tested her out earlier this morning. She's ready to go. But that don't mean you have to set any speed records."

I started the Cadillac and listened to it purr. "I wasn't planning to."

"Oh, one thing," he said. "The spare on the right side won't take air the way it should. I felt in there. Somebody put a boot on it and it didn't hold."

"What about the spare on the left side?"

"It's as good as gold."

"Then there's no problem. That's one more than I usually have."

"Wait a minute. I forgot something." Edgar opened the cigar box on his work bench and handed me a worn piece of paper. "It's the title. I found it in the glove compartment."

I felt my heart beat a little faster. I'd forgotten about the title. It might tell me more than I wanted to know.

I took it from him and examined it. Clinton Bass was the first owner. Doc Airhart was the second. If there was a third, I couldn't find it. "It looks like part of it might be missing," I said.

"Yeah, the mice got to it and built a nest with it."

"Do you still have the nest?"

He shook his head and walked away. "You've been working too hard, Garth. We both have."

I started home with the Cadillac. Rupert put on his red light and pulled me over before I'd gone a block. "I'd like to see your registration, please" was the first thing he said.

"You know I don't have one. I haven't had time."

"Your title then will do."

I handed it to him. He read it, then spat on the pavement, narrowly missing the Cadillac. "Interesting" was all he said.

"You going to write me up?" I asked.

"I should, for obstructing justice, but I won't."

"I appreciate it."

He took a slow walk around the Cadillac while I

waited. "She is a beauty, isn't she?" he said. "I've seen men kill for less."

I nodded, wondering where we were going with this.

He spat again, narrowly missing the Cadillac as before. "I saw Doc Airhart's name on the title. It's the last name, as I recall."

"Maybe so, maybe not," I said. "A mouse used the rest of it to build a nest."

"You have the nest?"

"Ask Edgar. He'll be glad to find it for you."

"After all the time you two have been putting in lately, I'm sure he will be."

"Anything on Woody?" I asked.

"Not on my end. That wrecking bar you found was clean."

"I found it in the creek. The water might've washed it off."

"I still can't figure what it was doing there."

"I can't either," I said. "Except . . ."

"Except what?"

"Except maybe Woody put it there."

"Why would he do that?"

"He wouldn't. Unless he had something to hide."

"What would Woody have to hide?"

I thought it over. I decided to tell him. "The Cadillac. I took it to Woody after I first found it. He was going to restore it for me."

"How long before he disappeared?"

"The day before. Then last Thursday Wilmer Wiemer and I were out that way. Somebody was inside his house. He also took Woody's pickup."

"Did he bring it back?"

"I don't know. I haven't been back out there to find out."

"You might have told me," he said.

"I tried to. But you were out looking for the pilot. Then I got busy with the Cadillac."

"That makes us both guilty."

"I guess it does. You found the pilot yet?"

"No. Not a trace."

"What about the marijuana?"

"That either. I'm about to give up looking. Another week, and it'll be too late anyway."

"Why's that?"

"It's not in the field anymore. We've had planes all over the county. We should've spotted it by now. That means it's hung up to dry. Probably in a barn someplace. In another week it could be ready to go on the street."

"But not the streets of Oakalla."

"So why bother, is that what you're saying?"

"It's a thought," I said.

"And one I've had," he answered. "I've never had much luck saving people from themselves. I wonder why I should start now. And if there weren't kids involved, I guess I wouldn't bother. Not as much anyway. But kids haven't lived long enough to make that choice, so I guess I'll have to try to make it for them."

"It's a losing proposition. The choice will always be theirs, no matter how hard you try."

"You know that. I know that. Ninety percent of the people in this business know that. But if you were in my shoes, what would *you* do?"

"What you're doing. I'd stomp every corn field in the county until I found it."

He spat again. This time he hit the Cadillac. "There's some comfort in that anyway."

He got in his car and drove away as I used my shirt to wipe off the tobacco juice. Then I drove home. Ruth met me in the alley behind the house. She didn't even let me get as far as the garage.

"Happy birthday," I said weakly.

She looked me straight in the eye. She didn't even smile. "I can't take it."

"Sure you can. It's a gift. You have to take it."

"What does that have to do with it?"

"Everything, damn it!" I was starting to lose my temper. First Rupert and now Ruth. You'd think I'd given her a dose of the black plague.

"I'm sorry, Garth. It's beautiful," she said. "In fact, it's the nicest gift anyone's ever given me, and I've seen some nice ones in my day. But I still can't take it."

"Why not, for God's sake?"

"It's too much. I'd always be in your debt."

"Forget that. There aren't any strings attached."

"There are always strings, Garth, whether you can see them or not. I'd never feel comfortable taking another dime from you again. And you might begrudge giving it."

"I won't!"

"You say that now. But it hasn't happened yet. And it won't happen if I have anything to say about it, which I do."

"Then I'll sell it to you."

"You know I can't afford what it's worth, and I won't pay less."

"I'll give you easy terms."

"It's no good. It's still worth more than I can afford."

By now I was exasperated. I was sore, dead tired, and out a week's work. Plus Woody was missing and Diana was in Madison. Poor me. "Then why in the hell did you ever say you wanted one?"

"Haven't you ever wanted something you knew you could never have? That's part of the fun of it. Once you have it what's there left to dream about?"

"I don't know, Ruth. And I honestly don't care. But say I keep the Cadillac in my name, will you drive it at least? Will you condescend to do that, or do I need to get down on my hands and knees?"

"What you need is a short vacation."

"Just answer my question."

She was trying to be patient but losing the battle. We were headed for a major confrontation.

110

"I won't promise you anything," she said. "You're the one who found the Cadillac in the first place, then hauled it all over town trying to get somebody to work on it before Edgar finally did. It's your idea, not mine. I didn't have word one to say about it."

The truth began to dawn on me. And I didn't like it. "You knew about the Cadillac, didn't you? You knew about it from day one?"

"What if I did?"

"And you knew all along you couldn't accept it as a gift?"

"I didn't think I could. No."

"Then why in the hell did you let me go to all the trouble to fix the God damn thing up?"

"Keep a civil tongue in your head. You don't have to swear at me. What was I supposed to do, ruin your surprise?"

"What surprise? The only one who's surprised is me! I've worked my ass off for the past week getting this thing ready and what happens? You tell me you don't want it! Well, I don't want it either! I was only doing it for you!"

"You can't shame me into taking it. So you might as well forget that."

"I'm not trying to shame you into anything!" I stopped for a moment. I was so mad I was on the verge of tears. Or hurt. I didn't know which. "Try to understand something, Ruth. I don't have many people I care for the way I do you. There's Diana and Rupert and my family, and that's about it. And Diana's not here, might never be here again, so it's hard to count her. What I'm saying is that there aren't very many people in this world for me to give things to. And when I do, it means something to me. It means a lot. Especially when it's something they've always wanted."

"I appreciate that. But you're missing the point."

"What then is the point?" I asked. "And damn it, now you're starting to sound like Diana!"

"That is my point. Diana's not here. I am. So you've put all your eggs in one basket, the Cadillac in this case, and given them to me. I don't want them. I don't want your fortunes to rise and fall with just me. That's too much to ask of anybody. You need another woman in your life, whether it's Diana or Whistler's mother. You'll be happier. I'll be happier. And we won't have to spend another morning like this."

"That's easier said than done. You don't go trolling for someone, like you do for walleyes."

"Some men do."

"Well, they're not me. If I've learned anything about relationships over the past twenty years, it's that they'll happen if they happen. You can't make them happen."

"That's my point exactly. You can't make me more than I am to you by giving me a Cadillac or anything else."

"I wasn't trying to make you more than you are to me."

"Then what were you doing?"

I threw up my arms and walked away. I didn't know, couldn't explain it to her if I did. We were both right, and we were both wrong. She read too much into the Cadillac. I put too much into the giving of it. I missed Diana. That was true. But even if she'd still been here, I would have given Ruth the Cadillac. With the same fervor and the same results and the same knot in the pit of my stomach? I doubted it. But then again, I was never very good at doing anything halfway.

I headed for my newspaper office. I'd neglected it long enough. It was time to get back to doing what I did best.

12

I spent the rest of the day working on this week's edition of the *Oakalla Reporter*. The mail had been coming in all week, and I had more opinions about Sniffy Smith than I did about marijuana. He was called everything from a fascist to a communist to the patron saint of Oakalla. Some wanted to fit him for a crown, others for a rope.

But as I tallied the letters, my respect for Sniffy grew. He at least had an opinion and wasn't afraid to state it. Almost everyone else, when they weren't condemning Sniffy, tried to walk the fence. They recognized the dangers of marijuana and also the inequality of the laws governing it and the enforcement of those laws. But that's as far as they went. When it came time to put up or shut up, offer a solution, they shut up and started listing statistics, as if that were the answer to everything. Too bad. I wanted to hear from their hearts. I heard from *Time* and *Newsweek* instead.

When I finished, I made myself a cup of instant coffee, walked to the window, and stood there watching the day unwind. Not much was happening in Oakalla on this lovely October afternoon. No one was walking the sidewalks, and the leaves had the streets to themselves. Every few seconds I'd see one fall and think *one more step closer to winter.* Maybe O. Henry had the best idea. Maybe we should paint at least one leaf on our window to carry us through until spring.

I called Ruth to tell her I was eating at the Corner Bar and Grill and wouldn't be home for supper. No one answered. That was strange. It was already five, and tonight was Ruth's bowling night. She liked to eat at six and leave at seven on the nose. Usually she was starting supper about now.

I waited fifteen minutes and called again. Again she didn't answer. She might still be angry with me and not answering the phone. But I didn't think so. Still angry, yes. But I never knew Ruth not to answer the phone. It might be one of her sources calling her.

At five-thirty I walked home. Ruth wasn't there. Nor was there a note telling me where she'd gone. I went back and discovered that both Jessie and Ruth's Volkswagen were there. The Cadillac, however, was gone.

I didn't know if I liked that or not. I was glad that Ruth had decided to drive it. After this morning it was more than I expected her to ever do. But she should have been home by now. Cadillac or no, she'd rather eat worms than miss a chance to bowl.

I waited at the window until six. I kept expecting to see her drive in at any minute with a full head of steam, enough to singe my ears for a week. I would have accepted that—to see her safely home.

At six I called Rupert. "No. We haven't had any accidents reported," he said. "What's the problem?"

"I'm not sure there is one. But Ruth took the Cadillac sometime today, and she's not home yet."

114

"Should she be?"

"I think so. It's her bowling night."

"Have you called any of her bowling buddies to see if she's there?"

"No. I'm just getting ready to."

"Well, if I hear anything, I'll let you know."

"Thanks, Rupert. I appreciate it."

I'd just hung up when I heard a car pull up out back. I hurried out the back door and was relieved to see the Cadillac sitting beside the garage, but it didn't look quite right. Ruth either. She sat behind the wheel without moving.

By the time I got to her, she'd started to get out of the Cadillac. She was bent over, moving slowly, and her face was the color of ashes. But when I tried to help her, she took a swing at me, the blow landing on my shoulder. She winced in pain. The effort hurt her more than the blow did me.

"Why won't you let me help you?" I asked.

"You've helped me enough for one day, thank you. Now get out of my way!"

"Where do you think you're going?"

"Bowling. Where else do you think I'd go on a Thursday night?"

"Over my dead body. You look like you belong in the hospital."

"Try to stop me and that's where you'll end up—in the hospital."

She limped past me holding her chest. I followed her into the house.

She sat down heavily at the kitchen table. It was as far as she could get at the moment. "You're not going bowling," I repeated.

"And you and whose army are going to stop me?"

"The condition you're in, I'll be enough."

"We'll see about that." She started to get up. She

115

changed her mind. "It's all your fault, you and that precious Cadillac of yours! Why aren't you out there seeing to it, instead of me? Seeing what I did to all your hard work?"

"Because I'm more concerned about you."

"That's a laugh. If you were so concerned about me, you'd never have waved it under my nose in the first place. You knew I couldn't resist driving it at least once."

"I hoped not anyway." I had to admit.

"Well, you can see where it got you. I've got cracked ribs, and it's got who knows what wrong with it. As if I cared."

"Are you sure cracked ribs is all you've got?"

"I'm sure. When Karl and I were still milking, I got kicked by a cow. It felt the same way—like I swallowed my chest."

"How do you know they're not broken?"

"Because I say they're not broken! That's good enough for me."

"I still think you need an X ray."

"You can think all you want. I'm not getting one. Besides, when you jumped out of that tree and sprained your ankle, you didn't get one either."

"I didn't get one because I knew they'd put me on crutches."

"So you limped around here for the next two months, complaining about every crack in the floor. Well, I'm about to return the favor. Now help me get up, so I can get into my bowling clothes."

"No. You're not going bowling."

"Then I'll do it myself." She started to get up and sat back down again. "You're right. I'm not going bowling. But I've got to go! We're in first place!"

"Why don't you get a substitute?"

"Who am I going to get at this late hour? I only know of one person, Sarah Sue Peters. And she can't even bowl her age."

"Maybe you can get a deferment."

"What do I want with a deferment? I already served my time. Forty years with Karl and then five and a half with you. That's enough service for anybody."

"I mean a bowling deferment. Maybe they'll let you make it up sometime later in the season."

"And maybe they'll let me sing at the Elks this Saturday night too. But I seriously doubt it."

"Why not?"

"Because Bertha Clendenning is president, that's why not."

"What does that have to do with it?"

"Her team's in second place. She'd be a fool to let me make it up."

"It's worth a try at least."

She thought it over. "Help me to the phone."

I helped her to the phone. Rather, I escorted her. She didn't want, nor need, much help. Meanwhile I went into the kitchen to see what I might fix for supper. I didn't see anything but leftovers. I liked leftovers about as well as I liked bologna sandwiches—twice a year at most, although I ate them a lot more than that.

"Well?" I asked on returning from the kitchen.

"I've got three days to make it up."

"Why only three days?"

"You'll have to ask her. I guess she figured if Christ could do it in three, I could too. Though the way I feel now, I've got a lot longer way to go." She got up and brushed past me on her way to the stairs.

"Where are you going?"

"To bed."

"Don't you want any supper?"

"Who's cooking?"

"I am."

"Would you want to eat your cooking if you were me?"

"Come on now, I'm not that bad."

"You're not that good either. Maybe I'll have some soup later. Right now all I want to do is lie down."

"Is there anything I *can* do for you?"

"You can get that Cadillac out of my sight. I doubt if I'll ever want to see it again."

"Any particular reason why?"

She stopped at the foot of the stairs. "Aren't cracked ribs reason enough? Or would you rather I'd broken my neck, which I very likely could have. Or had it broken for me."

"Is there something you're not telling me?"

"If it is, it's for your own good. Good night, Garth." She started up the stairs, moaning with every step. I watched her all the way to the top. When she finally got there, I wanted to crawl into the nearest groundhog hole and stay until spring.

I went back into the kitchen for one more look. I didn't see anything I wanted. I didn't have much of an appetite either.

I went out back to examine the Cadillac. It had a deep **V** on the front bumper and a few scratches on the hood, but other than that appeared to be all right. In fact, it seemed to have survived their incident a lot better than Ruth had. That bothered me, considering the pain she was in. And looking at it, especially now with the **V** in its bumper, it appeared to be grinning, as if the joke were on me.

I drove the Cadillac uptown and parked it along the yellow curb in front of the City Building. I was a member of the town board and had a key to the place. I also knew there was an empty stall in the garage right next to the firetruck. I hoped no one would mind if I parked the Cadillac there for a few days. More than anything else, I hoped we didn't have a fire.

From there I went to my office and called Rupert. "Ruth's home." I told him. "But it looks like she had an

118

accident in the Cadillac. I'll tell you more when she tells me more."

"Is she all right?"

"She thinks she might have some cracked ribs, but she won't go to the hospital for an X ray."

"How's the Cadillac?"

"In better shape than it has a right to be."

"Sounds like it's losing its charm with you."

"That might be."

"You don't happen to know where Ruth went today, do you?"

"No. I don't."

"When you do, let me know. When I was up in the plane today, I thought I saw your Cadillac over around Colburn. It could be Ruth stumbled onto something that she shouldn't have."

"You mean the marijuana?"

"It's possible. See if you can get her to talk about it, retrace her route if possible."

"Not a chance tonight. I'm lucky she's even talking to me at all."

"Then keep after her. It's important. We're running out of time."

"Maybe both of us."

"Would you mind explaining that?"

"When I can, Rupert."

I hung up and spent the next couple hours putting the finishing touches on that week's edition of the *Oakalla Reporter*. Then I called my printer in early and explained the situation to him. He understood why I wanted to be home. He said he'd take it from there, and if he had any questions, he'd call me. I doubted he'd have any. He'd been at this business a lot longer than I had.

I went home. It was too dark in the house, so I turned on a light in every room downstairs. Better. It made me feel less alone.

119

I went upstairs and stood for several minutes outside Ruth's door. When I didn't hear any noise from inside, I knocked on the door. "Ruth, are you okay?"

"Who wants to know?"

"Garth."

"I'm alive, if that's what you're worried about."

"That's what I was worried about. Do you need anything?"

"Some peace and quiet."

"Fine. I can handle that." I started to leave, then remembered something I'd been wanting to ask her. "Do you have any old yearbooks around?"

"What years?"

"Forty-six, forty-seven, somewhere in there."

"I've got 1947. My sister, Flossie, left it here along with a bunch of her other stuff when she moved to Arizona."

"That might do. Where is it?"

"In the bookcase in the spare bedroom. Bottom row, I think."

"Thanks. I'll take a look at it."

"Any particular reason why?"

"I don't have anything else to do."

"Besides that?"

"It was around that time that Woody Padgett graduated from high school. I think Wilmer Wiemer did too. From what Wilmer said, he and Woody go back quite a ways. He also said some other things about Woody. I just wondered if they were true."

"Such as?" She sounded better already.

"Later. When you're feeling better."

She didn't answer. She wouldn't give me the satisfaction of knowing that she was interested.

I found the yearbook and sat down in Grandmother Ryland's favorite rocker to read it. The first thing that struck me after the initial wave of nostalgia was the collective innocence on all of the faces in the yearbook. This was a generation that had just been through a depression and a world war, yet there was hardly a trace of cynicism showing. They still believed in themselves, their country, and the American Dream; that hard work, devotion to family, and faith in God were all you ever needed to be happy and prosper. They were wrong, of course. It was never that easy. But in no small way I envied them.

Though not all the faces were innocent. Nellie Brainard's, then Nellie Metzger's, wasn't. She wore the same cynical smile I'd seen on her portrait, the same smile I'd seen on the faces of other beautiful women who found the men in their lives somehow lacking. Though I'd been its target, I couldn't explain it. It was a longing perhaps for the knight on the white charger who spoke his lines fluently and never missed a cue. The perfect man. I'd met him once. He had a B.A. in philosophy, an M.S. in psychology, a Ph.D. in linguistics, and was a linebacker for the Los Angeles Raiders. He'd built his own log cabin in Maine, drove a Porsche, owned ten thousand shares of I.B.M., was a gourmet cook, taught ballet and skiing in the off season, and could tap dance while playing the Vienna Waltz on his Stradivarius. He was also six feet three inches tall and a eunuch.

I moved on to Wilmer Wiemer. His face had the smirk of cynicism too. It said he'd already seen the bottom line, and it meant a lot of long years at nine to five, even with benefits and early retirement. It said I'm smarter than that, and if there's a shortcut, I'm going to take it.

Then from Wilmer to Woody Padgett. With his quizzical look of bewilderment, even then Woody appeared the most innocent of all of his classmates. He reminded me of the blade of bluestem I found growing in Grandmother Ryland's corn field. It had once grown on virgin prairie—as high as a horse's back, she said. Somehow this one plant had survived years of cultivation, of planting and replanting, of harvest and reharvest, the binder, baler, reaper, and plow. And it had made its point, even if it didn't survive another season.

I looked for the list of achievements beside Woody's name. I didn't find many. He wasn't a joiner even then. The only thing he was a member of was the student body. An inactive one at that. He did have an interesting nickname, though: Possum.

I looked for Wilmer's nickname just to see if I'd read him right: Weasel. I couldn't have done better myself.

What about Nellie? Surely she had a nickname too. Everyone else did. Kitty. Somehow I was disappointed. Kitty seemed much too tame for Nellie. In one way. In another it seemed the perfect nickname. The iron fist beneath the velvet glove. Or in Nellie's case the sharp claws beneath the velvet fur.

I leafed through a few more pages. I wondered who Nellie's date had been for the Junior-Senior Prom. I shouldn't have wondered. She and Wilmer made a natural couple. They were both small and sculptured, and dressed in his white dinner jacket and black bowtie, he was almost as pretty as she was. Almost. Nellie had few equals. Here or anywhere else. And the stardust in Wilmer's eyes was proof of that.

I'd started to turn the page when I stopped and did a double take. Who was that beautiful blonde standing beside the stage drinking punch? I didn't remember seeing her in the rest of the yearbook. I leafed through it to make sure. No. She wasn't there.

I turned back to the prom pictures to look at her again. I'd been wrong in thinking that Nellie didn't have an equal here in Oakalla. The blonde wasn't as finely sculptured as Nellie, less of a work of art. Rather she was more handsome than beautiful, robust, whereas Nellie was sublime. But she was every bit as attractive. Even more so

122

to me. Perhaps because she seemed more open, and at the same time less accessible than Nellie.

"What's up?" Ruth asked, leaning over my shoulder. I was so intent on the blonde I hadn't heard her come in.

"You are. How come?"

"I couldn't sleep. You were making too much noise."

"I haven't said a word."

"That's the trouble. I could hear you thinking." She pulled up a chair beside me and gingerly sat down.

"How are you feeling?" I asked.

"Like someone shot me with a cannon. But better than I did earlier. What were you staring at?"

"Not what. Who. The blonde beside the stage. Do you know who she is?"

She smiled. "I'm surprised you don't. That's Thelma Osterday."

"You're kidding! Thelma used to look like that?"

"*I* used to look like that. Once upon a time."

"I didn't see her in the rest of the yearbook."

"That's because she graduated in 1946. This is 1947."

"Then what's she doing at the prom?"

"Drinking punch, it looks like."

"I mean whom is she with?"

"I don't know. Let me have a look at it." I handed the yearbook to her. She handed it back to me a moment later. "I still don't know. But I'd guess Woody Padgett."

"Woody is there?"

"I can't tell for sure. But it looks like the back of his head there to the right of Thelma. If there was a leaf growing out of it, I'd be certain."

"I thought Thelma and Woody were just old friends. I didn't know they dated."

"Learn something new every day, don't you?"

"Lately I have been."

"Both of us for that matter. I've learned to speak up before things get out of hand. If I'd told you in the first place I didn't want the Cadillac, maybe none of this would've happened."

"None of what?"

"Me running off the road. You getting hit over the head. Woody might even be back by now."

"I don't know, Ruth. I can't say one way or another. I am sorry you got hurt. I never intended for that to happen."

"Sorry enough to get rid of the Cadillac? Take it back where it came from?"

"Not quite yet."

She got up. It was a struggle. "Then you're not as sorry as you should be."

"How do you know it's the Cadillac's fault?"

"How do you know it isn't?"

"It might have kept you from getting killed today. If you'd been in your Volkswagen, who knows what might have happened."

"Probably nothing. Goodnight again. This time I mean it."

"Goodnight, Ruth. Sleep tight."

"I wouldn't bet on it."

I looked through the yearbook again. All the players were there—Woody, Wilmer, Nellie, Thelma—I just didn't know what the game was.

I closed the yearbook, leaned back in Grandmother's rocker, and rocked a couple times. I was wrong. Not quite all the players were there. The man I'd met at the Brainard mansion wasn't. I still didn't know who he was or what he was doing there or why he said he owned it. So far Ruth hadn't come up with anything either or hadn't told me if she had.

There was one other player I'd been avoiding. Doc Airhart. He knew more about the Cadillac than he was telling, and it didn't help to know that he was its former owner and that I'd found it on his property. Still, he seemed as surprised as I was when I found it. That was one thing in his favor. About the only thing. The fire at Edgar's had started shortly after Doc left me at the Corner Bar and Grill. That could be coincidence too. Again I doubted it. I felt like a banker who'd been stuck by his friend with a handful of bad notes. One of these days I was going to have to start calling them in. But not quite yet.

13

The next morning I got up early, fixed Ruth some coffee and toast, put them on a tray, and took them up to her. She was sitting up in bed, looking bored.

"Here." I tried to hand the tray to her.

"What's this for?" She wouldn't take it.

"I thought you might appreciate it."

"I do. But I'm just about to get up."

"You're not going to make things easy on me, are you?"

"Not if I can help it. Now if you don't mind, I'd like to get out of bed and get my robe on."

"What should I do with the coffee and toast?"

"Eat it before it gets cold. I'll be downstairs in a minute to fix my own."

I shook my head. "And you say I'm stubborn."

"You are. Next to Karl, about the stubbornest man

I've ever known. I don't know what I ever did to God to get two of you in one lifetime."

"Just because I won't get rid of the Cadillac?"

"It's just a symptom of a much larger problem."

"Which is?"

"You don't know when to stop."

"Thelma Osterday told me that just last week."

"Good for her. If enough of us tell you, maybe one of these days it'll sink in." She rolled her eyes and looked at the ceiling. "When pigs fly."

"I'll see you downstairs."

"Eventually."

A few minutes later she clunked down the stairs, complaining all the while. And I had the feeling this was just the beginning.

I ate my breakfast in silence, as she gimped about the kitchen fixing hers. When she finally had it all ready and sat down to eat it, she discovered she'd left her orange juice on the counter. She eyed it, then eyed me. It almost broke her heart, but she asked me to get it for her.

"Are you going to tell me what happened yesterday?" I asked, setting it in front of her.

"Why should I? If I do, you're liable to go off half-cocked and get yourself killed."

"Why don't you let me decide that?"

"Because I don't trust you, that's why. You think that because nothing's ever happened to you yet, it's not going to. You're bright about most things, but not about that. You haven't stopped to figure that all it takes is once."

"I always figure the odds. I don't risk my neck unless I think I can beat them."

"That's your opinion. I've got my own."

"I've managed so far."

"You see what I mean? You're a wide-eyed innocent when it comes to danger. Even Rupert will tell you that."

"Well, it's for Rupert's sake I'm asking."

"What do you mean?"

"I told you he was busy looking for a marijuana field somewhere in the county. Yesterday he was flying over Colburn and thought he saw you in the Cadillac. He thinks the marijuana is somewhere around Colburn. He believes you might have gotten too close to it, and that's why whatever happened, happened."

"He might be right," she admitted.

"But he won't know, will he, unless you tell me what happened."

"Why don't I just tell *him?*"

"Because he's not home," I lied. "I tried to call him earlier."

"Why don't we wait until he gets home?"

"Because I don't know when that'll be. And by then it might be too late. Rupert thinks the marijuana is already out of the field and in a barn somewhere. Anytime now it might be ready for the street. That could be as soon as today."

She sighed. "I might as well tell you. You'll worm it out of me one way or another anyway—then will you be satisfied?" She shook her head. "Never mind. It's like asking a leopard to change its spots."

She stopped a moment to take a breath. I saw her wince in pain. I could tell it hurt her to breathe too deeply. "It never would've entered my mind to go over there. Not until you dropped that Cadillac in my lap and went off in a huff because I wouldn't take it. I figured I'd kill two birds with one stone—check up on something and soothe your ruffled feathers a little. So I took the Cadillac and went over to Woodhollow."

"Woodhollow! Why did you go there?"

"I'm getting to that. I went through Colburn and began to wind around, and before long I didn't know where I was. But I just kept going and eventually came to Woodhollow. I don't know what I was expecting, but that wasn't it. It doesn't look like a sanitarium to me, more like a place where a rich old man might live."

"How is a sanitarium supposed to look?"

"Alive for one thing, like there's somebody living there. Though Cousin Ada warned me that might be the case."

"Cousin Ada?"

"Cousin Ada. You remember that big man with the small red ears you asked me about, the one that looked like a walrus? Well, I put out the word to my relatives about him and Cousin Ada phoned me yesterday morning from Colburn. She said it sounded an awful lot like the man who used to run Woodhollow Sanitarium, though she was sure they'd closed the place down a few years ago. But she said it wouldn't hurt to check, so that's what I did."

"Has Woodhollow closed down?" I asked.

"From all appearances it has. I must've been there an hour before I saw anyone at all. Then I saw a woman walking a dog. A poodle of all things! A little white one that kept stopping at every tree. They were coming my way when I heard something, looked up, and saw a man coming down the road toward me. A little man with a white shirt and dark skin. He looked like a Mexican to me."

"What did the woman look like?"

Ruth glared at me. She hated to be interrupted. "I never did see her face. She was too far away. But she was small and slim like Nellie Brainard used to be."

I did a double take. "Are you saying it was Nellie?"

"No, I'm not. I'm saying she was small and slim, like Nellie used to be. I haven't seen her in over thirty years."

"Then why did you bring up Nellie?"

"I didn't. You did. Anyway, I remember you asking about her. You and Liddy Bennett."

"Liddy Bennett? What does she have to do with it?"

"A week ago Tuesday night somebody stole a loaf of bread and a jug of milk from her. Liddy saw the person leaving. At a distance and in poor light. Liddy said that if she didn't know better, she would swear it was Nellie

Brainard." Ruth's look was questioning. "But that's not possible, is it?"

"I'll let you know as soon as I know. For now I'm more interested in what you found out about the walrus."

"Not much at the moment. But Cousin Ada is working on it. His name is Abram Davids, if that helps any. He's been at Woodhollow as long as Cousin Ada can remember."

"Is he still at Woodhollow?"

"I don't know. I left before I got a chance to find out."

"Why did you leave?"

"I was scared, that's why. The way that Mexican was coming down the road toward me, he wasn't looking to sell me some pumpkins. I didn't know what he was after, but I had the feeling it was me."

"Did you leave the same way you came in?"

"No. I was headed the other direction. I didn't take the time to turn around. I figured if I could find my way there, I could find my way home again. I was wrong. I got lost. I wandered around for about a half hour before I saw this farmhouse and lane. I decided to go down the lane and ask directions. I knew before I ever got to the house nobody'd be home. It had that look about it. I was right. Nobody was home. I turned around and came back out of the lane. It was just about then I noticed the pickup following me."

"What kind?"

"I don't know. It never got that close. But it was red. I remember that much."

"You're sure? Woody owns a red pickup."

"I know. It looked a lot like his."

"How much like his?"

"Too much like his."

"Go on." I'd think about that later.

"I drove on. I didn't think too much about it at first, not until the pickup kept making every turn I did. I sped up to see what would happen. I gained ground on it for a moment, but a couple of minutes later there it was right behind me again."

"Did you see who was in it?"

"No. I was too busy driving. This went on for several miles, me winding around the country, not knowing where I was, and it just sitting there behind me like a bur on a dog's tail. Finally I got mad. I decided to get rid of it once and for all. I was on a gravel road at the time, and I figured if I could stir up enough dust, he wouldn't be able to see which direction I turned when I came to a crossroads. Or at least it'd slow him down long enough for me to get away from him. So that's what I did. I put my foot to the gas and dared him to keep up with me. Then I saw a T coming up. It was perfect. I was coming down a hill; the T-road was asphalt, and by the time he sorted it out, I'd be miles down the road. But the Cadillac had other ideas. I hit washboard just before I got to the T, and when it came time to turn, I couldn't. It was like the Cadillac had made up its mind to go straight ahead, and that's what it did. The next couple of minutes aren't very clear. I remember going over an embankment. It looked like Grand Canyon on the way down, but not quite as steep on my way back up it. Grass and leaves were flying everywhere. Then this tree jumped out in front of me and that was that. The next thing I knew I was bouncing off the steering wheel."

"What happened to the pickup?"

"I don't know. I was too busy counting my ribs to look."

"Do you think he saw you crash?"

"I wouldn't want to bet one way or another. I'd raised a lot of dust. My guess is he made the turn and went on."

Either that or he didn't want to get involved in an accident, and the questions that would follow. "What happened then?" I asked.

"I took inventory, saw I was still alive, started the Cadillac and backed it away from the tree, drove up the embankment, and came home."

"Just like that?"

"Just like that. It couldn't have taken more than a minute."

"You must've been in shock."

"When your backbone is connected to your rib bone, I don't know what else you'd call it."

"You're lucky you weren't hurt worse."

"It wasn't because the Cadillac didn't try. It's got a mind of its own, just like that junk heap of yours. Except yours is just contrary. That Cadillac's something else again."

"You liked it the first time you rode in it."

"That was 1936, Garth. A lot of changes since then—in it and me both."

"You might be right."

"Louder. I didn't hear you."

"I said you might be right."

Her eyes rolled upward. "God, you're my witness. He admitted it for once."

"But not because it has a mind of its own," I added. "Not because it has a soul. Any more than Jessie does."

"What then?"

"I don't know. I'm in the process of finding out. Do you think you could direct me to the farmhouse where you turned around?"

"I couldn't find it myself. How can I direct you?"

"Would you recognize it if you saw it again?"

"In my sleep. It'll probably keep me up at night."

"Why's that?"

"It's spooky, that's why. That whole area around Colburn is. It's desolate and run down and practically deserted. I can't put my finger on it. It just gives me the willies." She gave me a questioning look. "You're not thinking of going over there, are you?"

"I thought I might."

"I thought this little exercise was for Rupert's benefit. To help him find the marijuana growers."

"It is. It's for mine too. I'd like to know who was following you and why."

"You've changed your tune. That's not what you told me to begin with."

"I'll tell Rupert where I'm going, if that'll make you feel better."

She struggled to her feet and walked to the phone. "You'll do even better than that. You'll take Rupert along." She dialed his number. Elvira, Rupert's wife, answered. I could hear her from where I was sitting. She said Rupert wasn't home. He was up in a plane somewhere, had been since early this morning.

Ruth hung up and tried to stare me down. "You're not going," she said. "Besides that, you lied about calling Rupert earlier."

"I'll be fine."

"You'll never find it on your own."

"That's the chance I have to take."

"Not good enough," she said. "I'm going with you."

"You can't."

"Why not?"

"Because of your ribs, that's why not!"

"I helped put up a thousand bales of hay with cracked ribs, and milked a dozen cows morning and night. I can surely ride in a car. Even yours. And don't tell me it's too dangerous. Any fool knows that. At least this fool knows when to cut and run. I'm not so sure about the one I'll be riding with."

"I still don't like it."

"Of course you don't. It cramps your style. That's why I'm doing it. It's better than sitting here wondering if I'm ever going to see you alive again."

"Okay. I won't argue."

"Good. You'll save us both some breath."

An hour later we were on our way. Ruth was fortified with two pillows, one to sit on, and the other to hold up against her chest just in case. Even at that, she winced at every bump in the road and kept a steady eye on Jessie's speedometer to make sure I didn't go too fast. Every time I got above forty-five she'd cough, and I'd slow down again. I never realized until then how much fun it was to have all three of us in the same car together.

"Comfortable?" I asked.

"What do you think?"

That was about the extent of our conversation.

Overhead the sun was a veiled red, as a white skein of clouds began to unravel and float in streamers across the sky, pushed by a warm south wind that drove the leaves ahead of it and left them in brown drifts along the road. I drove southwest toward Colburn and right into the wind.

Colburn was once a mill town, then a railroad town, then a bedroom town, now nearly a ghost town. Consolidations had closed its schools; the powers that be had closed its churches, and bankruptcies had closed its businesses. As a kid I used to like to come here with Grandmother Ryland and wander about the grain elevator while she got feed for her chickens. It was alive then, and in the hustle and bustle of Saturday morning seemed the only place on earth to be.

Not so today. We bumped along its crumbling streets, past house after empty house—fallen porches, broken windows, and a bush growing inside a front door. Then a mangy dog wobbled down the street toward us carrying a half-eaten rabbit. I saw Ruth shudder. I felt the same way.

Once we got past Colburn, Ruth directed me as best she could. At all costs I wanted to avoid Woodhollow. I was saving it for another day.

We came to a T-road. "Which way?" I asked.

"Your guess is as good as mine. It all looks the same to me." Then she had a second thought. "Wait a minute! Is that an Angus bull over there?"

"I'd say so. He looks too content to be a steer."

"Never mind. I shouldn't have asked. Take a right here. I came back this way yesterday."

134

I came to a side road. "Which way now?"

"To the right. To the left is the embankment I went down."

"Do you want to stop?"

"Why should I? I know what it looks like."

I took a quick glance before we turned right and started up the hill. Ruth was right. It did look like Grand Canyon from here. It might have been a good thing she hit the tree. No telling where she would have ended up if she'd kept on going.

I thought about the Cadillac sitting safely back in Oakalla, while here we were, driving straight into danger. Somehow it didn't seem right. In her heart I knew Ruth felt the same way.

We found the farmhouse about a half hour later. I turned down a narrow lane that was deeply rutted with a ribbon of grass growing down the middle of it. It hadn't seen much use lately. The yard looked scraggly from neglect and the white farmhouse hadn't been painted for years. All of which led me to believe the place was abandoned.

Ruth stayed where she was. I got out of Jessie and walked to the house. A rotted wooden stoop served as the front porch. I stepped on it gingerly, hoping I wouldn't break through, and knocked on the screen door. I managed to rouse a couple of drowsy flies from the inside glass. That was all. I shaded my eyes and peered inside. I didn't see anybody.

I tried the inside door. Its round smooth knob felt slick in my hand. I had a hard time gripping it. But when I finally applied enough pressure, the door opened grudgingly. It scraped the floor all the way inside.

I hesitated before going in. The house had a thin acrid smell that leaked out at me and left a sour taste in my mouth. There was a large rust stain on the ceiling and a hole in the floor where it had started to rot. No furniture that I could see. Only a beige wall phone directly across the room from me. That posed an interesting question. If no one lived here, why was there a phone?

I went inside. The place was deserted and had been for some time. Even the cockroaches had left. But the phone looked almost new. I picked up the receiver and got a dial tone. Suspicions confirmed.

I went back outside. Ruth was waiting for me at the door. "You ready to go?" she asked.

"Just about."

"Well, hurry up. My nerves are starting to jangle. I'll breathe a lot easier when we're out of here."

I couldn't argue with that. I didn't like the feel of this place either. It didn't look like a family farm, but at the same time it was cultivated. And its corn crop was about the poorest I'd seen lately. Which, along with the phone in the house, meant they might be growing something else besides corn.

I looked at the tobacco barn that was partially hidden by a thick stand of weeds. Grey and paintless, it leaned to one side and looked ready to topple in the next gust of wind. "Turn Jessie around." I said. "And keep the motor running."

"What are you up to now?"

"Go ahead. I'll just be a minute."

I walked to the barn. There was a padlock on both ends, but I was able to squeeze between the boards enough to see inside. One look told me it wasn't tobacco drying in here. It was marijuana. Lots of it. Enough to pay somebody's bills for a long long time.

I didn't waste any time getting out of there. I didn't know how often they checked their crop, but this one looked ready for delivery. I didn't want to be part of the shipment.

I got in Jessie and immediately thought about all the things that could go wrong with her, that had gone wrong with her in the past. I hoped she realized her danger as well. Because if worst came to worst, I planned to leave

136

her here. She didn't even sputter when I put her in gear. She must've read my mind.

"Find something interesting?" Ruth asked.

"I'll tell you later."

We left the lane and turned east. We hadn't gone a half mile down the road when we met a red pickup coming our way. It was coming fast, leaving a huge cloud of dust in its wake. I tried to catch a glimpse of the driver but had no luck. All I saw was paint and glare. And dust, so much I couldn't see to drive. I pulled to the side of the road and stopped.

Ruth's eyes were watering, as she held her chest trying not to cough. "Are you okay?" I asked.

She just glared at me.

"Is that the pickup that followed you yesterday?"

She nodded.

"It looks like Woody's."

She nodded again.

"Are you curious to see where it's going?"

Another glare. This one designed to turn me to stone.

"I didn't think so."

When the dust finally settled, I put Jessie in gear and took off again. I would have liked to have known who was in the pickup and where it was going, but I couldn't risk it with Ruth along. Especially not when she had cracked ribs. Not in Jessie anyway. That was asking too much. I didn't want to use up all my luck in one day.

"There were two of them in the truck," Ruth said about a mile later.

"Did you recognize either one of them?"

"No. I was lucky to see what I saw."

"More than I saw," I admitted.

She tried not to smile. But it wasn't in her.

The first thing I did when we got home was to thank God. The second thing was to call Rupert. He wasn't home yet, but I tracked him down an hour later. I told him what I'd found in the barn. He was in a hangar clear across the

137

county, but he said he'd get there as soon as he could. I told him to bring reinforcements. He said he would.

Ruth meanwhile turned on the television, sat down in her easy chair, and propped her feet up. I noticed an electrical cord leading from the wall socket to the back of her chair. She was resting on the heating pad.

"Thanks for going along today," I said. "That took a lot of guts."

She ignored me. She was concentrating on the television.

"What's that?" I asked her.

"*I Dream of Jeannie*. It's a rerun. It was just on last week."

"You couldn't prove it by me." I started to leave. There was someplace I wanted to go.

"Where are you going?"

"For a walk."

"Supper's at six."

"I'll be there."

"Garth?" She stopped me at the door. "You're not short on guts yourself. Sense maybe, but not guts. You've got more than enough for two people."

"Thanks, Ruth. I needed that."

14

I walked to Thelma Osterday's. If Woody was involved in drug dealing, I needed to know that. If he wasn't, I needed to know that too. It might tell me where to go from there.

Thelma wasn't home. At least she didn't answer her door when I knocked. I went around back and looked in her garage. Her car was gone. I wondered for how long.

I went through the back door into the kitchen. I saw a deck of cards sitting on the kitchen table, along with an orange sugar bowl and blue salt and pepper shakers. Beside the cards were a pencil and a running scoresheet. T was ahead of W by about three hundred points. I didn't know for sure the game they were playing, but I guessed it was gin rummy.

I heard a car pull up in back. It looked like Thelma's. She got out, then reached back for a sack of groceries. I decided I really didn't want her to find me here. After our encounter at the Brainard mansion, it might be hard to convince her I wasn't spying on her.

I planned to walk out the front door, circle the block, and come back. But on my way out of the kitchen, I nearly tripped over something that changed my mind. It was a case of Coke. On top of it was a box of Snickers. I no longer wondered where Woody had gone when he left the Marathon a week ago Monday. He'd come here. Even though Thelma said he hadn't.

I stayed where I was. To Thelma's credit she didn't throw the groceries at me when she came in the door. She didn't even scream. She looked like she might even have been expecting me.

"So we meet again," she said, setting the groceries down on the sink.

"It looks like it."

"You're trespassing. You know that, don't you? I have every right to call the law on you."

"You have every right, but I don't think you will."

"Why not?"

"Because you need me to find Woody. I'm the best bet you have."

"I don't need you for anything, Garth. Now I'd like for you to leave."

"You need help, Thelma. Why don't you admit it?"

"Because even if I did need your help, I wouldn't admit it. You used to be my friend. Now you're just a damned nuisance. Now get out!" She took a skillet from the wall. She looked like she meant to use it.

I did as she asked. She was a big woman and could no doubt swing a mean skillet. But I stopped at the door. "Why? That's all I want to know."

"Why what?"

"Never mind. I'll just say something we'll both be sorry for."

"Go on," she said. "I want to hear what's on your mind."

140

"It's not worth it, Thelma. We're already on the bottom rung. Our friendship doesn't have much further to go before it's gone."

"I'll think less of you if you don't tell me than if you do."

I smiled at her. "I didn't think that was possible."

She didn't smile back. "Go on. Speak your mind. Then get out."

"Okay, I'll speak my mind and get out. See that case of Coke and that box of Snickers over there? Woody bought them at the Marathon a week ago last Monday when he went in to have his oil changed. When was the last time Woody had his oil changed? He always changes it himself. So he was either in a hurry or didn't care about the cost. Or both." I hesitated. This was the hard part. But I didn't see any way around it. "My guess is that Woody thought he was coming into some money. That's why he let someone else change his oil for once. I'd also guess he had a trip planned. That's what the Coke and Snickers are for. My final guess is that he planned to take you along. Otherwise what would the Coke and Snickers be doing still here?"

"And where did Woody plan to get all this money he was coming into?" she demanded.

I dropped the bomb I'd been holding. "From the sale of marijuana. About two tons of it."

She looked at me with disbelief. She'd forgotten all about the skillet. It hung limply in her hand. "You'd better sit down, Garth. You've been out in the sun too long."

"There's more. Yesterday over around Colburn, Woody's red pickup followed Ruth for several miles. She had an accident trying to get away from it. She was lucky she wasn't killed. She was hurt badly enough the way it was. Today we took a drive over to that same area where the pickup started following her. You'll never guess what we found. A barnful of marijuana.

That seemed to deflate her. She took a seat at the

141

table, setting the skillet down in front of her. "You saw Woody's pickup, you say?"

"Ruth did yesterday. Then we both saw it again today."

"And you didn't try to follow it?" She sounded more confused than angry.

"Would you have, under the circumstances?"

"No. I guess I wouldn't have, thinking what you think. But you're wrong about Woody. He'd never do what you're saying."

"And Wilmer wasn't here a week ago Monday and Tuesday?" I guessed that's where he'd been the nights I saw him.

"What if he was? What does Wilmer have to do with it?"

"My guess is that it's Wilmer's money you're using to buy the stuff. You plan to send him his share later on after you make the sale.

"And where are we getting the *stuff* as you call it?"

"From whoever's growing it. Whoever hit me over the head last Tuesday night. My guess is that he and Wilmer had a meeting set up. I showed up at the wrong time."

"If what you say is true, then where is Woody? Why haven't he and I taken off by now?"

"Maybe he got double-crossed. Maybe the grower took Wilmer's money, killed Woody, and kept the marijuana. It's happened before, when amateurs have gotten in with the pros."

I couldn't read her face. Whatever her involvement, she was having some doubts of her own. "Okay, say everything you've told me is true. Why would Woody and I do such a thing in the first place? We don't lack for anything. Why take the risk?"

"That's the part I can't figure out."

"When you do, please let me know. Until then keep you thoughts to yourself. Otherwise I'll sue you for every dime you've got."

142

"You wouldn't get much."

She smiled sadly. "From either one of us."

I walked home. I wasn't very proud of myself. I'd shot from the hip at Thelma, intending to shake her up, which I had. The trouble was I couldn't prove a thing I'd said. I didn't know how much of it I believed myself. That bothered me, that and the fact I'd also lost a friend.

After supper I took a walk just to unwind. Someone had a wood fire going and I stopped to smell it. It brought back memories of those Octobers years ago when we'd crowd around the fire with our wiener sticks and marshmallows, drinking in the smoke and fellowship.

Never once did I toast my marshmallow to a golden brown like the rest of the gang. I never had the patience. I stuck mine right in the flame and then blew like hell once it caught fire. The result was a gooey black lump that stuck to my lips, burned my mouth, and tasted like a fireman's boot. And once the long-awaited hayride started, never once did I find any treasures under the hay—unless I counted straw mites. Innocence. It must've been good for something.

"Rupert called" was the first thing Ruth said when I came in the door. "He left a number."

I dialed the number Ruth had written down. It rang several times before Rupert answered.

"Where are you?" I asked.

"At the farmhouse where you sent me."

"Did you find the marijuana?"

"No. It was here, no question about it. But it's gone now. We did find something else though." Judging by the sound of his voice, it wasn't good.

"What was that?"

"A dead man."

"Woody?"

"No. The pilot I told you about. I'd guess he's been here about a week."

"You found him inside the barn?"

143

"No. We found him outside—by accident. Clarkie stumbled over his grave when he went to take a leak. He wasn't buried very deep."

That made me think about Woody, the shovel in his barn with the dirt still on it. Maybe he wasn't buried very deep either, nor very far from the barn.

"Any idea who killed him?" I asked.

"No."

"You think he was part of the deal, then got cold feet and tried to pull out? Maybe that's why he called you and told you about the marijuana."

"It looks like it. In any case he's got clay feet now. Dead men tell no tales."

"I'm sorry it worked out that way."

"So am I, but I'm not about to give up. They had to take the marijuana someplace. We'll just keep looking until we find it."

"If it's still around."

"I imagine it is. They didn't have time to take it very far."

"Unless they took it to an airplane."

"For now we won't consider that possibility. Anyway, thanks for your help. I'll take it from here."

"Are you saying you don't want my help anymore?"

He paused for maximum effect. "I'm saying the pilot was carrying a gun. He never got the chance to use it."

"It sounds like the other side plays rough."

"Either that or they're spooked. In either case it's a good situation to stay out of it."

"I will if I can," I said.

"Why can't you?"

"The red pickup we met today, the one that followed Ruth yesterday, I think it's Woody's."

"You think Woody's involved in this?"

"I don't know what to think. I'll work at it from my end; you work at it from your end, and maybe we'll meet in the middle."

144

"Just don't forget what's your end and what's my end," he warned.

"I won't." Though I couldn't promise that.

"I guess you're old enough to know what you're doing."

"I wish I were."

As I hung up, I noticed Ruth standing in the doorway. "Well?" she asked.

"We left none too soon today."

"I heard."

"I'm sorry for getting you into this."

"Don't feel like you didn't have help. I didn't have to go over there yesterday."

"It might not have made any difference."

"How so?"

"It depends on what they're really after. They might have come looking for us eventually anyway. In that case it was a good thing you did go over there. It gives us a head start."

"Then what are they really after?" she asked.

"I don't know. Maybe the Cadillac."

"Then let them have it."

"It's not that easy."

"Where you're concerned, it never is."

15

At the crack of dawn Ruth and I arrived at my newspaper office, armed with an electric coffee pot and a package of cinnamon rolls. She started with 1950, I with 1945, reading back issues of *Freedom's Voice*, the forerunner of the *Oakalla Reporter*. We read in separate rooms, mainly because she had the habit of reading out loud whenever something interested her.

We'd been at it for about two hours when she walked into my office, poured herself a cup of coffee, got a cinnamon roll, and sat down heavily in a chair, holding her ribs as she did. "I give up," she said. "There's nothing, absolutely nothing, in here that could possibly be of interest to anyone, living or dead. Unless, of course, you *want* to know who attended Millie Rothenberger's graduation on Sunday, May 10, 1953. And exactly what they were wearing down to their shoelaces. And what they ate. And who their second cousins were and how many old maid

aunts they had. And that their parakeet was named Birdy."
She stopped to wince and catch her breath. "You having
any better luck?"

"No."

"You plan on giving up?"

"No."

"I didn't think so. Were you always this stubborn?"

"Almost always. I just remember my old rabbit hunting days. You kicked a hundred and ninety-six brush piles
and no rabbit ran out. The hundred and ninety-seventh,
the one you didn't kick, had a rabbit in it. Or at least you
always thought it did."

"And that's supposed to cheer me up?"

"Just finish your roll and get back to work."

I'd found something of interest. It was the September
19, 1947, edition. Maynard Troxel, an itinerant farm
worker, had been killed by a hit-and-run car along Fair
Haven Road early in the morning the fourteenth of
September. I counted backward five days. That would be
on a Sunday morning. Passersby on their way to Fair
Haven Church had found the body. An investigation was
underway at the time.

I read the subsequent issues to see if the car had ever
been found, but the incident was never mentioned again.
Either they'd fast lost interest in itinerant Maynard Troxel
or someone had put a lid on the case. It could have
happened either way. Oakalla then, as now, was known for
taking care of its own.

I continued reading until I came to the March 19,
1948, edition. This edition told of the accident that killed
Nellie Brainard's parents, Marvin and Eunice Metzger. On
their way to Fair Haven Church they went off the road and
hit a culvert. Eunice was pronounced dead at the scene.
Marvin never regained consciousness and died two days
later. Daughter Nellie, at home, was the only survivor.

"Ruth, come in here!"

She appeared in the doorway. She looked a little pale

for her efforts. I'd forgotten she still wasn't her old self yet.
"Yes, Bwana, what is it?"

"I've got something I want you to read."

"You mind if I sit down?"

"Sure. You can sit in my chair."

I handed her the paper and she read the article about the Metzgers. "So?" she asked.

"It says daughter Nellie *at home.* I thought she was away somewhere."

"She was." She read the article again. "It does say that, doesn't it? Maybe she came back early."

"From where?"

"Wherever she was."

"Do you have any idea where that might have been?" I asked.

"I've heard rumors," she said. "As I told you before, some say she was sent to a girls' school down South, while others claim she was closer to home."

"How close to home?"

"Woodhollow Sanitarium."

"Then how did she get out of there?"

"I guess they let her out. Unless, of course, she ran away. But I never heard of anyone looking for her."

"Would you do me a favor?" I asked.

"As long as I can do it at home. My chest hurts, my eyes are crossed, and *The Big Valley*'s about to come on."

"Abram Davids. I know Cousin Ada's working on him but I want you to hurry her along. We've neglected him long enough."

"Do you think he might have something to do with this whole business?"

"I don't know, Ruth. At this point I'm not ruling anyone out."

She hesitated before leaving. That wasn't like her. Usually I had to tie her down to keep her here, and the minute I cut the rope she was gone.

"Was there something else?" I asked.

"Do you mind driving me home?"

"No. I don't mind. Are your ribs really hurting you?"

"It's not my ribs. It's the dream I had last night."

"Was I in it?"

"No. I was. I was dead, if you want the long and short of it. I didn't like the feeling."

"It was just a dream. Don't forget that."

"Don't try to talk me out of it. You're not the one who had it."

I drove her home and went inside with her to make sure everything was all right. Then I returned to my office and made a call to the Court House. Nothing that surprised me. The Brainard estate was still in Nellie's name.

I began reading where I left off. In the April 16, 1948, edition I found something else of interest—a quitclaim deed. It read: "C. L. Brainard to Dr. W. T. Airhart, forty acres, Madison Township, for services rendered." Services rendered? I got up and looked at the Adams county map hanging on the wall. The farm where I'd found the Cadillac was right in the heart of Madison Township. I had to wonder.

I poured myself a cup of coffee, ate a roll, and went back to work. Eventually I'd have to confront Doc. But considering the way things went with Thelma Osterday last evening, I could wait a little longer.

Bang! The photograph jumped out at me and caught me by the throat. There was the Cadillac in a full-page ad for the Jackson Highway Garage. The caption read, "Special Cars Need Special Treatment."

Pictured with the Cadillac was an older man, probably in his late fifties, with ears the size of side-mirrors and the polished look of someone who has spent most of his life posing. Pictured with him was a young woman and two unnamed mechanics, who, though they looked like they couldn't overhaul a rollerskate, were the real heroes of this ad.

I took a closer look at the young woman. Even though the photograph didn't do her justice, I was sure it was Nellie Brainard. There was no mistaking her brooding face, the eyes that could pierce concrete.

But something had changed in Nellie. The last remnant of softness was gone. She was only Kitty in one sense of the word. She reminded me of the cat Grandmother Ryland once had, a cream-colored female and one of the prettiest cats I'd ever seen. But she never raised a litter of kittens. Grandmother said it was because she was sterile. I didn't understand until I saw Cream sitting in the barn, calmly licking herself, while her abandoned litter lay dead and dying a few feet away. I realized then that nature wasn't perfect, that some of us are born with a sterile heart.

I looked at the date of the photograph. August 13, 1948. 1948? For some reason that year was too familiar to me.

I walked to the City Building, went into the garage, and looked at the license plate on the Cadillac. 1948. I thought I remembered it.

So now what did I know? I knew that Big-Ears Brainard, if that's who it was in the photograph, owned the Cadillac as late as August 1948. I also knew that along about that time he took a drive from which he never returned. If the Cadillac had been in the barn since 1948 and Big-Ears had driven it to the barn himself, then could he be very far away? A good question. It depended on whether he was alive or dead. And if dead, for how long?

I went home, picked up a shovel and my metal detector, put them in Jessie, and drove toward the old barn where Doc Airhart and I had first found the Cadillac.

My one hobby as a boy was coin collecting. It all started when my great-uncle died and left me a small bag of Indianhead pennies. I bought a book to see what they were worth and in the process discovered that the change in my pocket might be worth something too. Since I was a paper boy at the time and had access to a lot of pockets, I started collecting. I went at it hard and heavy for about six years, then lost interest, partly because the good coins were starting to dry up and partly because I went away to college and needed every coin I could get my hands on.

I'd never started collecting again, but about two years ago I had bought a metal detector, mainly because it was always there when I could spare a minute, and it took me out and away from town to some long-forgotten settlement where not even Rupert could find me. It wasn't a paying proposition. Not when I counted gas, time, mileage, and the price of the metal detector itself. But it sure was a hell of a lot of fun. And when I dug down and found my first Mercury dime, I couldn't have been happier than if I'd struck gold.

I parked Jessie in the abandoned lane and walked toward the barn. The bright fall colors had passed their zenith and were now fading toward brown; but holding fast, still clinging stubbornly to their hues, were the ambers, deep reds, and purples—rich and subtle colors whose time had finally come.

I went into the barn, set my shovel down, and turned on the metal detector. I fine tuned it until all the static was gone and began sweeping it back and forth across the floor of the barn. I was waiting for the beep that would tell me I'd struck pay dirt. It wasn't long in coming, as the needle jumped in agreement each time I swung the metal detector over the same spot.

I held it steady a moment to make sure it didn't reject whatever was there. When it didn't, I got down on my hands and knees and began to dig with my hands. I didn't get very far. The dirt floor of the barn was packed like concrete, and my fingers soon felt like I'd stuck them in a fan.

I'd picked up the shovel when I saw an old corn knife wedged between two boards. I used the knife to dig and in a short time unearthed what appeared to be a silver tie clasp. I wiped it clean with my shirt and checked for

151

initials. C.L.B. Colonel Louis Brainard? Charles Lawrence Brainard? Chicken Little Brainard? There were endless possibilities. No certainties.

I searched the rest of the barn and came up empty. Then I moved outside and made a sweep around the barn. I found several rusty nails and one rusty horseshoe. I threw the horseshoe over my shoulder for luck. Threw it the wrong way and found it again a few minutes later.

I was starting to lose interest. I'd swept the whole area around the barn and still no sign of Big-Ears Brainard. I was searching for the pocket change that he might have brought with him the day he disappeared. If the change stayed in his pocket and the pocket stayed with Big-Ears, even if the pocket had long since rotted and the change had fallen out, chances were good that Big-Ears wouldn't be far away. At least that was my assumption. So far it didn't amount to much.

I widened the search area and kept on going—mainly because I didn't know what else to do. The silver tie clasp told me that Big-Ears had once been here, dressed in his Sunday best. What it didn't tell me was when. If he once owned this property, as the quitclaim deed indicated, it could have been 1948 or 1926 or any time in between. I had no way of knowing.

I came to a small depression at the same time the metal detector began to beep. And the signal was strong. I bent down and began digging with the corn knife. I should have stopped when I came to my first rusty can. But it took me six more to get the message. I'd just found the farm's dump.

I stood up and brushed the dirt from my jeans. There were at least forty acres here, and I didn't have time to sweep them all. Besides that would be like looking for a needle in a haystack. I was never good at finding needles in haystacks.

I shut the metal detector off and began walking toward Jessie. Tomorrow was Sunday. I could get out here early and give it another go. Maybe by then my luck would have changed.

I came to the open well that Pete had nearly driven into. I looked in the well, then looked at the metal detector. What the hell. It was worth at least one shot.

I eased down into the well, making sure the ground under me was solid. It was. That was a relief. I didn't plan to do jumping jacks, but I didn't want to wake up in China either. I'd fallen through the ice once and nearly drowned. That was enough incentive to always look before I leaped.

I turned on the metal detector and swept it over the bottom of the well. I got a signal, but it was faint and unclear. That meant that whatever was beeping was buried deep. It also meant I had to climb back out of the well after the shovel.

Five minutes later I stood with the shovel in hand, staring down at the hole I'd made. With each shovelful the signal had grown stronger, and so had the air around me. It had the thick taste of death and decay. And putrification. Too thick to swallow, it caught in my throat and stayed there.

Actually it was the gold in his teeth, not the change in his pocket, that set off the metal detector. He lay about two feet down, grinning up at me showing off his dentures, while I leaned against the side of the well, trying to keep my cinnamon roll down.

I hadn't done a textbook job of digging. I was halfway through his femur when I realized it wasn't a root I was chopping on. Then I had to find which end of him was which without doing any more damage, and that meant digging the last six inches by hand. And now that he was uncovered and I'd proved how clever I was, I'd just as soon have shoveled the dirt back in and forgotten about him.

I looked around the farm. Everything seemed in order. The squirrels were busy gathering their winter supply of nuts; the birds saying quiet good-byes before heading south. They sky was blue, the day mellow. Not a sign of evil anywhere. But I felt immersed in it, that if I didn't get out of this hole soon, I was going to drown.

I walked back to Jessie and took the old Army blanket out of her trunk. I shouldn't be doing this. I should drive to the first phone, call Rupert, and turn the body over to him. That was the safe, sane, and prudent thing to do. But Rupert was looking for marijuana and who knew when he'd get around to me. Whenever it was, I wasn't sure I could wait that long.

It wasn't easy getting him onto the Army blanket. I couldn't just take him by the hand and drag him on. That meant I either had to take him piece by piece or scoot the blanket under him and hope for the best.

Once in my childhood I'd flippantly called someone an "old bag of bones," never thinking I'd be called upon to regret that remark. But I did now. Because by the time I got done scooting and scooping and swearing and sweating blood, that's what I had for my efforts—a bag of bones. I could have gone in with a steam shovel and saved myself the trouble.

I put the blanket and bones in Jessie's trunk and started back toward town. I felt like a messenger of doom, like the news I brought would not be welcome and would significantly and irreparably alter the life of a dear old friend.

16

I parked in front of Doc Airhart's. I didn't get out right away. Instead I sat in Jessie sorting my thoughts. Finally I got out and took the blanket from Jessie's trunk. Like the line from the song, I'd come too far to turn back now.

I knocked on the front door. Doc opened it and let me in. I didn't speak to him. I walked through the house and down to the basement, where I set the blanket on his pool table.

He opened it up and took a look inside. He showed marginal interest, that of a physician who'd seen more than his share of old bones. "Friend of yours?" he asked.

"I never saw him before."

"Where did you find him?"

"In your well. About fifty yards south of the barn where we found the Cadillac." I'd dropped the bombshell. Now I wanted to see what the fallout would be.

Not much. He just looked at me and raised his brows

as if to say I told you so. "Does Sheriff Roberts know about this?"

"Not yet, he doesn't."

"Do you plan to tell him?" he asked.

"When the time comes."

"What are you waiting for?" He looked at me. His blue eyes were never brighter, nor more intense. I couldn't face them. I looked away.

"He's busy at the moment, looking for marijuana."

"So what do you want from me?"

Again I had the chance to challenge him. Again I failed to do so. "I'd like to know who he is. And if possible, how he died."

"How soon?"

"As soon as possible."

He held up the skull and looked at it. I thought I saw a subtle shift in his stance. His interest no longer seemed merely clinical. "Check back with me sometime later this afternoon. I might have something for you then."

"Thanks, Doc. I appreciate it."

He didn't hear. He was too busy with his own thoughts.

I went back to my newspaper office, sat down on my swivel chair, and had a long talk with myself. If I could, I would have quit now, driven the Cadillac back to the barn, put the bones back in the well, and let bygones be bygones. But I couldn't. Something inside me wouldn't let me. Nor would something outside me. "Let sleeping dogs lie" Doc had warned. I should have listened to him. I had the feeling the dog was now awake and on his way to my door.

Ten minutes later I sat in the lobby of Oakalla Savings and Loan, waiting for Wilmer Wiemer. Or rather for Wilmer's secretary who was keeping a close eye on me. But I enjoyed waiting—especially for doctors and lawyers and dentists and in tax lines and shopping lines and travel lines, wherever the decor was inspiring, the company charming, and somebody else's time always more valuable than mine.

Thirty seconds later I admitted myself to the inner sanctum of Oakalla Savings and Loan. I didn't wait to be buzzed but went directly to Wilmer's door and walked in.

He didn't look up right away. I wondered if he was going to. Then he flashed his hundred thousand dollar smile, and I was suddenly glad I'd borrowed my money elsewhere. Wilmer was a chameleon. Maybe not at heart, but in all outward appearances. I never knew from one day to the next whom I'd find wearing his skin. I imagined his wife, Elizabeth, had the same problem.

"Come in, Garth!" Easy, since I was already in. "What brings you here to my door?"

"Business as usual."

His smile began to fade. He wasn't sure how to take that.

"Relax, Wilmer," I said. "If I were going to blackmail you, I would have by now."

He smiled slyly, sure he had the winning hand. "I don't know what you're talking about."

I wanted to teach him a lesson. I pretended to reach into my shirt pocket for something that wasn't there. As I did, I discovered something that was there—a piece of paper. What could that be? No matter. I'd get to it later. "Maybe this tape will refresh your memory."

Wilmer did a double take, then gave me a genuine smile. "You had be going there for a minute, Garth. I keep forgetting you don't have a price."

"I have a price, Wilmer. You just don't have the means to pay it."

He relaxed, leaning back in his chair. "So what do you want today? I've told you all about me I'm going to. More than I wanted to."

"You didn't tell me why you were after the Cadillac."

"What Cadillac is that?"

157

"*My* Cadillac. The one I had down at Edgar Shoemaker's. The one you looked in on two nights in a row."

"Oh, *that* Cadillac!" He studied me shrewdly. He wanted to see just how much I did or didn't know. "What's it worth to you?"

"A good night's sleep, for one thing."

"That's all?" He sounded disappointed.

"Seriously, Wilmer, what could I give you that you don't already have?"

He looked at me, then looked away. His eyes had said, "A friend." Wilmer said, "I'll have to think about it."

"While you do, will you give me some answers?"

"What exactly do you want to know?" he asked.

"The Cadillac. Why are you interested in it?"

He paused just long enough to make me wonder. "I'm not. I'm interested in what might be in it."

"Which is?"

"A million dollars. Give or take a hundred thousand."

"How do you know it's there?"

"I don't. But I looked everywhere else. I figured it had to be there."

"Why don't you start at the beginning?" I asked.

"There's no beginning to start at. I worked at the bank my first year out of high school. Big-Ears Brainard came in one day with a fist full of thousand-dollar bills he wanted to trade in on new ones. He came in every day after that for two weeks, always to a new teller so we couldn't get an exact count of just how much he was trading in. But I kept my eye out for him and when it was all over, I had a pretty good idea. Then it wasn't a week after that he disappeared. I figured Nellie had done him in and that was that. I'd never see that money again. But it wasn't long before I changed my mind. For one thing, Nellie stuck to that mansion like a bur to a long-haired dog. Why, unless she was afraid somebody else might find what she hadn't? For another, if Nellie had the money, she'd have spent it like the sailor she was. So then later when she disappeared into the blue without a word to anyone, I figured she might've given up and moved on. In that case, I still had a chance at it. So I grabbed a shovel and went out there looking like everybody else."

"But you never found it?"

"That's obvious, ain't it, Garth? If I had, I sure as hell wouldn't be here."

"Where would you be?"

"Treasure hunting, I think. Somewhere off the Florida coast. Where I could be out and about and still be warm. I wouldn't be sitting around here getting old and fat. You can bet your ass on that."

I had Wilmer pegged right. He, like me, was a buccaneer at heart. He hunted for gold. I hunted for truth. But for both of us it was the search, not the find, that was most important. And perhaps for both of us life's real treasure was waking up where you wanted to be with someplace you wanted to go. Except for those you loved, nothing else much mattered.

"And you don't think Nellie ever found the money either?" I asked.

"Her or anybody else. Or I'd have known about it."

"Which leaves the Cadillac," I said.

"Which leaves the Cadillac. Except you and Edgar have had it apart and back together again and you didn't find the money either. Or did you?"

"No. I wouldn't be asking if we had."

"And Edgar wouldn't still be smoking those dime cigars of his."

"So where is the money?" I asked. "Do you think Big-Ears took off with it?" If so, whom had I found in the well?

"I didn't then. I might now. I thought I saw him once about thirty years back. I didn't give it much thought because by then I was sure he was dead."

"Where was that?"

"The Brainard mansion. I was out there nosing around after dark, looking for the money as usual, when I saw somebody digging a hold in the yard. I yelled at him, told him to get his ass out of there, thinking I could scare him off and have the place to myself. It didn't work. He started after me with a shovel. From every indication he intended to use it on me."

"And you think it was Big-Ears?"

"Could have been. There was something familiar about him."

"It wasn't Woody, was it?"

"Possum? Why do you ask that?"

Why did I ask that? Something my brain knew that it wasn't telling me made me ask. "I don't know. It just popped into my head."

"No. It wasn't Possum. I'd know him anywhere. But it's funny you'd ask because I always thought that he was the ghost everybody saw and heard out there. It probably didn't start out that way, but that's the way it ended up."

"Any particular reason why you say that?"

"Possum had a thing for Nellie. It started in high school. Anything she wanted done, Possum'd do for her. He was too dumb to know she was using him, at least too dumb to know what to ask for. Otherwise he could have had her like some of the rest of us. Such as she was."

"How was she?"

"Hungry. Too hungry for me to ever satisfy her."

"Nellie was a nymphomaniac?"

"No. Nellie was something else again. I never did figure what. I'm not sure there's a word for it. Nellie wanted more than your pecker. She wanted your soul, lock, stock, and barrel. And to be honest, just to get in her pants again, I almost gave her mine."

"How was that, Wilmer?"

"She wanted to kill her parents. She wanted me to help her."

"Which you didn't?"

"No. But I thought long and hard about it. Then when they went off Fair Haven Road and were killed a year later, I thought about it some more. Nellie, you see, had come home in the meantime."

"From Woodhollow?"

"I'd guess that's where she was."

"And you think Nellie killed them?"

"I think she could have. And never thought twice about it."

"Do you think Woody helped her kill her parents?"

"I never thought he had it in him. But I've been wrong before. He hung around there a lot after Big-Ears disappeared. And even after Nellie left, I'd see him sneaking out there long about sundown to mow the place. Or early in the morning before anyone was up. Whatever his reason he was sure cozy about it. He's also the one who told me Nellie went back to Woodhollow."

"Woodhollow Sanitarium? What was she doing there a second time?"

"Beats me. Living there I guess."

"As a patient?"

"What else? I went over there a couple times to see her, but I never could get past the fat man that used to run the place. He said Nellie didn't want any visitors. But I know for a fact that Possum talked to her on several occasions. He as much as told me he did."

"What did you want with Nellie?"

"To strike a deal. Even if there isn't any money on it, that estate of hers is choice property. Somebody ought to be doing something with it. It might as well be me."

"But you never got a chance to talk to her?"

"Nope. Like I said, the fat man wouldn't let me through the gate."

"How long ago was that?"

"Nine, ten years ago. I've heard since they've closed the place down. Good riddance. That's what I say."

"You sound like you carry a grudge."

"I do. But not because of Nellie. Over the years the fat man tapped me for more money than I thought Wood-

hollow was worth. He seemed to cater to a particular clien-
tele, old and rich. Some of them happened to have their
money with me."

"What about Nellie, is she old and rich?"

He laughed. "Unless she found Big-Ears' money,
which I don't think she did, she doesn't have a dime."

"What about the estate? It's still in Nellie's name. At
least that's what the county clerk told me this morning."

"It's still in her name," he assured me. "Last time I
checked anyway. But all she owns is the land there where
the mansion is. Big-Ears sold off the rest while he was still
alive."

"Then how could she afford Woodhollow?"

"You'll have to ask the horse's mouth himself, Davids I
think his name is. He has an answer for everything. I'm
sure he'll have one for you. That is, if he's still around."

I planned to do that as soon as I had the chance.

"Which brings us to another matter." I saw his face
harden. I didn't wonder how he'd made it this far in the
business world. He could be affable one moment and
granite hard the next—whatever he needed to be.

"Which is what, Wilmer?"

"Your business and my business. Where your business
ends and my business begins. You seem to have had a lot of
trouble with that line lately."

"Go ahead. I'm listening."

"I had a call from Thelma Osterday last night. Now
Thelma's not one to get too excited about anything, but
she was excited last night. And mad. At you. At me. At the
whole damn world, if you want the truth of it. And I can't
say I blame her any, considering what you put her
through. Accusing her and Possum of heading up a drug
ring with me as the money man. Me I can understand. I
won't say I never thought of it. But her and Possum?
That's like putting the finger on Minnie and Mickey
Mouse. Whatever possessed you anyway? Normally you
know where your head is at."

162

"You don't have time to hear all of it."

"Well, I've got time to hear some of it! You've been getting a lot of answers from me. I'd like to hear some of yours."

I didn't know how much to tell him, mainly because I didn't know how far I trusted him. Wilmer never played a trump, unless he intended to take the trick. And he'd played a lot of trumps so far today. That probably meant he had more up his sleeve.

"What's it to you?" I asked.

"What do you mean, what's it to me? You accused me of dealing drugs! I'd damn straight like to know why!" He sat up straight in his chair. He looked at least six inches taller.

"I'm getting close to something, right?"

"I don't know what you're talking about."

"Then you won't mind telling me what you were doing at Thelma's on Monday and Tuesday night last week?"

"There you go! Asking the questions again! I was playing gin rummy, and that's the God's truth! Thelma can't sleep any better than I can. It helps the night go faster."

"Or why you've been looking for Woody?"

"Thelma asked me to, as a favor to her. Besides that . . ." He caught himself. He almost said more than he wanted to.

"Besides what?" I asked.

"Nothing. If you aren't smart enough to figure it out on your own, I'm not about to coach you."

"Does it have something to do with the Cadillac? You were in the neighborhood the night Edgar's shop caught on fire. You didn't happen to see who started it, did you?"

Wilmer suddenly got busy with some papers on his desk.

"Did you, Wilmer?" I persisted.

"I think we've had our say, Garth. You'd better quit while you're ahead."

"Ahead of what? I'm not sure I know any more now than when I came in here."

"Then that's your fault. I've told you all I know."

"Have you, Wilmer? Whom are you protecting? Yourself?"

"No! Goddamn it! I'm not a firebug! The last thing I'd do is set fire to that car!"

At this outburst Wilmer's secretary looked in on us. He waved her back to her desk.

"Then whom are you protecting?"

"A friend of yours. So just forget it, huh?"

"It's Doc Airhart, isn't it?"

I could tell by Wilmer's reaction that it was.

"Do you know what he has against the Cadillac?" I asked.

"I've heard rumors. But why don't you ask him?"

"What kind of rumors?"

"That Big-Ears Brainard had something on him. That Doc sold the Cadillac to him for a dollar. Big-Ears got drunk one night and was bragging about it. That's what I heard."

And except for my loyalty to Doc, I had no reason to doubt him. I stood and looked at Wilmer for a long time, so long he grew uncomfortable under my gaze.

"You still don't believe me, do you?" he asked. "You don't believe a word I've said."

"I don't know what I believe anymore, Wilmer. I wish I did. It might help if you'd tell me why you were looking for Woody and why you want Paul Black's farm. Then I'd really know you were shooting straight with me."

He didn't answer. Instead he stood, took me firmly by the arm, and showed me to the door.

17

I drove to Doc Airhart's and knocked on the front door. When he didn't answer right away, I went inside. I found him in the basement studying the skeleton I'd brought him. He picked up the skull, examined it, and set it back down again. He was humming to himself, strutting his stuff like an old bantam rooster who knows he still has it after all these years. I hated to be the one to burst his bubble.

"What's the verdict?" I asked.

"The verdict is, I don't know," he answered. "He might have died from natural causes. He might have been poisoned or smothered. I have no way of knowing. Maybe somebody else does, but I don't. Not without a lab and more time than it's worth. Still then I might not know. I do know he wasn't shot or cracked on the head or run over with a car. He only had one broken bone and that came earlier on in life. I'd say about ten years before he died."

"You have any idea who he is?"

"Some. I'd guess his age at about late fifties or early sixties. That'd be about Big-Ears Brainard's age when he drove off into the blue and never came back. And Big-Ears stepped in a hole and broke his ankle while chasing a stray softball at a church picnic. I know because I was there and set the ankle myself. And it had to be before the War because I never set foot in a church afterward. So you can take it from there."

"But you're sure it's Big-Ears?"

"Not proof-positive. I wouldn't bet my life on it. Maybe my house though."

Knowing how well Doc loved his house, he was proof-positive. "Do you have a guess as to what happened to him?" I asked.

"Your guess is as good as mine. I'd like to hear yours."

"I asked first."

Doc smiled at me. He usually knew what I was about. "What are you doing, giving me a chance to confess?"

"Something like that. If one is in order."

"Do you really think I killed him?"

"I think you might have had a reason."

"Which is?" he asked.

"Late in 1947 a man was killed by a hit-and-run car along Fair Haven Road. It had to be between the church and town because some people found him on their way to church. That might make it somewhere in the neighborhood of the Brainard estate. So if it was and Big-Ears Brainard knew about it, he just might put the squeeze on whoever did it. He might even force him to sell a 1936 Cadillac convertible for a dollar."

Doc looked at me, then down at Big-Ears. "Actually, it was five dollars," he said. "Big-Ears never could keep his figures straight."

"But it happened as I said?"

"Pretty much. I was on my way home from visiting a sick friend, if you know that old story. I told my wife,

166

Constance, that I was going to the hospital, which happened to be in the other direction. My mind wasn't on my driving. Besides that I hadn't had much sleep. I didn't see the man at all. I only heard the Cadillac hit him. I stopped and got out, thinking it was a dog. When I saw that it wasn't and he was already dead, I got back in the Cadillac and drove on. I wasn't worried about me. But there were others to protect. Big-Ears saw me drive by. He put two and two together and came up with blackmail. He wouldn't say anything if I'd sell him the Cadillac for a reasonable price. I asked him what a reasonable price was. He said a dollar. I said I wouldn't sell it for less than ten. We finally agreed on five. And if you want to know the truth, Garth, I've always felt I got off cheap."

"And it ended there? He didn't try to squeeze you for more money?"

"Why should he? He was worth a lot more than I was then."

"Did anybody else know about it?"

"About the accident? I'm sure they did. Or at least they guessed. But nobody ever came forward. They probably figured they needed me more than they did the dead man. And in the long run they did. Right or wrong and harsh as that might sound."

"Then you didn't kill Big-Ears Brainard?"

"Why should I? He had all he wanted from me. I had no reason to."

"But you did start the fire in Edgar's shop?"

"Who told you that?"

"Wilmer. He had his eye on the Cadillac, too—for other reasons."

"I started it. I don't know why, except to try to warn you off. I knew Edgar was right there in the kitchen. I never intended to burn his shop down. And if I did, well then I'd just build him another one."

"Why were you trying to warn me off?"

167

"I told you before, that Cadillac's poison. The sooner you get rid of it, the better."

"No other reason?"

"What other reason would there be?"

"What about that forty acres Big-Ears deeded to you? That was the next spring, seven months after you hit the man along Fair Haven Road. What was that for?"

Doc's face hardened. "Spite."

"I don't understand."

"I don't expect you to understand."

"What aren't you telling me, Doc? Why did Big-Ears give you the forty acres?"

"Because he knew I wanted it, that's why. Once he got the knife in, he wanted to twist it a little."

"What knife is that?"

"The Cadillac! I thought you'd been listening. He thought it'd break my heart to give it up. When it didn't, he found another way."

"What way was that?"

"The forty acres!" Doc was losing his patience with me. "Big-Ears knew I wanted it . . . so bad I'd give almost anything for it. . . ." His voice trailed, lost the force of its conviction.

"Go on, Doc. I'm listening."

"That's all I'm going to say."

"For services rendered. Big-Ears gave you the land for services rendered. What were the services, Doc?"

"You know everything else. Why don't you tell me?"

"I'd rather not say what I'm thinking."

"What are you thinking?"

"I'm thinking of the seven months that passed between the time you hit Maynard Troxel and the quitclaim deed was filed. I can remember only one thing. The Metzgers ran off Fair Haven Road and were killed."

He spat on the floor; his ears turned red. I'd never seen him quite so angry. "What are you saying, Garth? That I sold out to Big-Ears? That I deliberately falsified a medical report? Why in God's name would I want to and why in God's name would he ever ask me to? What were they to him?"

"Nellie's parents. He married her shortly after that, remember? Would they have approved of her marriage to Big-Ears?"

"Not if they had any sense, they wouldn't! But that's no reason for him to kill them, or for me to help him!"

"It is if he wanted Nellie badly enough, and if you wanted the land badly enough. As you said, too much of anything corrupts. Including beauty."

He shook his head sadly. He was disappointed in me. "That's the craziest thing I ever heard. I thought you had more sense than that."

"Then why don't you ever go out there—if you love the place so much?"

"Because every time I do go out there I'm reminded of what happened! That the only reason I own it is because I cheated on Constance! And killed a man in the process!" His voice softened. "And betrayed the two things I valued most in life—the love of my wife and the Hippocratic oath. In eighty years I've only made two vows. I broke them both the same day." He turned away from me. There were tears in his eyes. "That's too high a price to pay for anything, no matter how lovely it is."

He stared at the wall of his basement, seeing every crack and chip and stain. He seemed to be examining his own life at that moment, too aware of his own imperfections, yet man enough to live with them. "If you want the truth of the matter, I aborted Nellie's child," he said quietly. "Big-Ears said it wasn't his and that even if it was, he didn't want it. The last thing he needed was a squalling brat around."

"What about Nellie, did she want it?"

"She never said one way or another. She just lay there in that huge bed, staring at something I didn't want to see. If it hurt her in any way, she never let on. I might as well have been working on a fence post. She was such a beauty too. It seemed a terrible waste."

"Of what?"

"Nature, in its most sublime state. If there's anything more beautiful than a beautiful woman, I don't know what it is. But to give beauty all out of proportion to feeling . . . I don't know how to answer that one, Garth."

Neither one of us did. "Was Maynard Troxel the lever Big-Ears used on you?" I asked.

"Yes. The Cadillac wasn't enough for him. He needed one more favor. Nellie's abortion."

"Then what was the deed for?"

"That was just Big-Ears' way of doing things. He knew how much I wanted that land. He made damn sure I'd never get the chance to enjoy it."

"He sounds like a nice man."

"He was a prince, believe me."

"Why didn't you just tear up the deed?"

"Why don't you just give up the Cadillac? I gave you fair warning from the start about it. I damn near burned down a man's business to make my point." He turned back to me. His anger had flared again. "But no, you're determined to hang on to it come hell or high water. Well, you're going to see both before you're through. Take it from someone who knows." He folded up the blanket with Big-Ears Brainard's bones inside and handed it to me. "And while you're at it, take yourself and your friend and be on your way. I've seen enough of Big-Ears Brainard for one lifetime." He was pushing me toward the stairs. "And for what it's worth, I don't have the faintest idea what killed the Metzgers. I was flat on my back with the flu at the time. But since you do, I suggest you look in that direction, and until you come to your senses, leave my door alone."

I trudged up the stairs and went outside. At this rate I wasn't going to have to buy any Christmas presents.

I put Big-Ears back in Jessie's trunk, then drove to my

office, and began reading what I'd read earlier. Something had stuck in my mind, something important that I was missing, but I couldn't remember what it was.

I read until my eyes began to cross, then got up and walked around the room a couple of times before I called Ruth to tell her I'd be late for supper again. Outside it was sunset. The sky was orange and blue, the wind still, the trees along Gas Line Road tucked in for the night. I leaned against the screen and took a deep breath of the outside air. It smelled cool and dusty, as a thousand memories came rushing in as one—of past Octobers and those who shared them with me. I sighed and went back to work.

One hour later when I finally did see what I'd been missing no one was there to strike up the band. I sat with my head on the desk, wondering how I could have missed it in the first place. Not that it would have changed anything. But at least I would have had a hot supper.

It wasn't an article I was looking for. It was the photograph of Big-Ears and Nellie and the two unnamed mechanics standing beside the Cadillac. And even then I didn't see the connection. Not until I realized that Woody Padgett was one of the mechanics.

I called Thelma Osterday. She answered on the fourth ring. She sounded out of breath, like she'd just come in from outside. "Thelma, this is Garth. Don't hang up. I know you want to, and you probably have a right to, but don't."

"Go on. I'm listening."

"I need some answers."

"Don't we all. Why should I give them to you?"

"Because you want Woody back. So do I. And I'm your best bet for getting him back alive."

"I thought you said yesterday he was dead."

"I said he might be. I didn't say he was. It depends on what he's involved in."

"He's not involved in anything. I told you that."

"Then why is he still missing? And why are you

171

running to answer the phone? You have to trust somebody, Thelma. It might as well be me."

She thought it over, then said, "Fire away. But if you get off the track once, I'm hanging up."

"Fair enough." Even though I didn't know what the track was. "Last week you said that Nellie Brainard ruined the best man this town ever raised. You were talking about Woody, weren't you?"

"What if I was?"

"When did it happen?"

"When did *what* happen?"

"Nellie and Woody?"

"It never happened," she answered, "at least not in the way you're thinking. Nellie strung him along, getting every ounce of work out of him she could. He didn't get much in return."

"What did he get in return?"

"I'm not sure I want to answer that."

"It just seems strange, that's all, that Woody would keep up the Brainard place all these years. It was Woody, wasn't it?"

"Who told you that?"

"Wilmer Wiemer. Though not in so many words."

"Wilmer never did know when to keep his mouth shut."

"So it was Woody?"

"I won't say it was. I won't say it wasn't."

"Why not?"

"That's my business."

"What about the ghost of Big-Ears Brainard? Could that have been Woody, working late at night?"

"You're just full of questions, aren't you?"

"I'm afraid so."

"It might've been. That's all I'll say."

"That isn't much."

"Some days you have to take what you can get."

"Then one last question. Do you know where Woody went last Monday after he left you?"

"No. He didn't say."

"Do you have any idea?"

"I've racked my brain. I can think of only one place."

"Where's that, Thelma?"

"I won't tell you. Not yet anyway."

"What are you waiting for?"

"I'm sorry, Garth. That's my business."

"Have you heard from Woody since he's been gone?"

"No. Not a word."

"Do you expect to hear?"

"I did at first. I'm not so sure now."

"And that's all you'll tell me?"

"For now. You should be happy with that."

"I am. Thanks, Thelma."

I hung up. I smiled as I did. At least Thelma and I were back on speaking terms again. And all because I stayed on the right track.

I called Ruth at home. "Your supper's in the oven," she said. "You can eat it when you get here."

"That's not why I called. Do you have anything on Dr. Davids and Woodhollow yet?"

"I'm working on it. Cousin Ada's supposed to call back tonight."

"What about Wilmer? Does Aunt Emma know why he wants that land where Woody lives?"

"No. But I think she's hot on the trail. She's even hired a couple surveyors with her own money."

"Why?"

"I didn't ask. I figured she'd tell me in her own good time."

"Well, let me know as soon as you hear."

"I plan to." She noticed my pause. "Was there something else?"

"Diana didn't call, did she?"

"No. Were you expecting her to?"

"No more than any other night. Thanks, Ruth."

"I'm sure if there's a phone line that runs from there to here, there's one that runs from here to there."

"I tried it once. It was busy."

"Try again. You might get through this time."

"Maybe tomorrow."

"It's your life." She hung up.

I called Rupert. He was home for once. "Yes, Garth, what is it?" he asked.

"How'd you know who it was?"

"I've got a trouble light that blinks on every time it's you. Besides, I just sat down to supper."

"I should be so lucky."

"You usually are. What's on your mind?"

"How goes your search and destroy?"

"It goes. That's about all I can say."

"Are you getting closer?"

"No. We're not any closer than we were ten days ago. Clarkie thought he saw that red pickup you told us about, but it gave him the slip."

"Where was that?"

"In the Colburn area."

"How far from Woodhollow Sanitarium?"

"I'd say a mile or two. Why do you ask?"

"I'm just playing a hunch. Do you have time to do me a favor?"

"Depends on what it is."

"I think Nellie Brainard was committed to the Wood-hollow Sanitarium twice. The first time in 1947. The second time in the early 1950s. I'd like that first date confirmed. I'd also like to know who had her committed the second time."

"Tomorrow's Sunday," he said. "I plan on taking all of it off. I owe it to Elvira and myself. But I'll make some calls for you tonight, if you like."

"Thanks, Rupert. I'll call you back in the morning."

"Not before nine."

174

"I'll try to remember."

"Anything else?" he asked. "So you don't call again."

"There is one thing. I've got a bag of bones in Jessie's trunk. I think they belong to Big-Ears Brainard."

He sighed heavily. "Will they keep until morning?"

"I don't see why not. They've kept for a long time now."

"I'll send Clarkie after them then." He paused. He really didn't want to ask, but felt it was his duty. "Anything else I should know?"

"Not at the moment. I'll keep you posted."

"See that you do."

I got in Jessie and drove out to Woody's. It was a sweet still night, heavy with dew and the scent of harvest—the kind of night you like to share with someone special. I drove with my window down, taking in all that I could. Because one day soon it would all come to an end. The wind would turn east, then north, pushing ahead of it a cold rain that stripped the leaves and picked the petals from the last aster. And I'd sit staring out of my window, wondering where autumn had gone.

Woody's place looked just like I'd left it—the aging barn still standing on borrowed time, the door of his house open to all comers, the surrounding woods black and still and somehow threatening. I got out of Jessie and went inside the house. After fumbling for a light switch on both sides of the door, I finally found one and flipped it on. An overhead light came on, and I felt suddenly vulnerable, like if anyone was out there, he could see me a lot better than I could see him.

I shut the light off, went back outside, and took my flashlight out of Jessie's glove compartment. I turned it on, shook it once, then turned it on again. Better. If I could get close enough, say within two inches, I could read a billboard.

I went back inside the house and began searching through Woody's things. He kept most of his papers

175

stuffed in the bottom drawer of his chest. It didn't take me long to see that I wasn't the only one to have been in here recently.

Bills, like leaves, pile up in order, the oldest ones on the bottom—unless someone comes along and starts raking through them. Then they all get mixed together, and you have to sort the whole pile if you're looking for one in particular.

Someone had mixed up Woody's bills. I looked through the rest of his drawers. They, too, looked like they'd been shuffled. Even the floor had recent scratches, like someone had been trying to pry up the floor boards.

I went back to Woody's bottom drawer and began sorting through his bills. A window here, a shingle there, a pound of nails everywhere told me that Woody had done a lot of repair work over the past few years. One look around his house told me that it hadn't been here.

I searched the rest of the house. Finding nothing of interest, I petted the pink poodle "Won at Frank's," turned off the light, and went out to the barn. It, too, had a searched look. White showed in the floorboards where someone had been prying away at them, trying to get leverage, and the hay mow had a mussed look, like Grandmother Ryland's used to when we kids would get done playing in it. And the bale I'd left on the floor was back in the mow, as if someone had forgotten whether they'd knocked it down or not.

But Woody's tools were all in place—except for the wrecking bar I'd found in the creek. I picked up the shovel with the dirt on it. If it could talk, I'd bet it could tell me all I needed to know.

I stopped by the City Building on the way home. I went in the front door and used my flashlight to find the Cadillac. I didn't want to attract any more attention than I already had.

Edgar said he'd had trouble getting air into the right

spare tire because it had a boot in it. I had to wonder if it had anything else in it.

I pulled the tube out of the tire and examined the boot. It looked like a home-repair job to me. I peeled off the boot and found a long slit in the tube. Nothing else. Nor was there anything besides air in the left spare. At least it didn't rattle when I shook it.

I was disappointed. I thought for sure I'd find Big-Ears Brainard's fortune. That meant it was never here or someone had beaten me to it. Either one was a good possibility.

18

On my way down the stairs the next morning, I heard someone running across the living room. I stopped to listen. I heard it again. It came in bursts, like squalls of rain.

I stopped at the foot of the stairs and watched, as Ruth took three quick steps and threw an imaginary bowling ball. Her release was fine, but she was a little stiff on her follow-through.

"What are you doing?" I asked.

She blushed. Even her green house slippers turned red. "None of your business."

"It looks like you're bowling to me."

"What if I am?"

"I just wondered why."

"Because I don't want to get out of practice, that's why."

"You only missed one game."

"It's been ten days since I bowled last."

"Well, you've still got four days to go. You don't bowl until Thursday. What's the rush?"

She didn't answer that question. She looked guilty, but I didn't know why. Before the day was out I'd know, and kick myself for not thinking of it sooner.

"By the way," I said. "Did Cousin Ada ever call about Woodhollow Sanitarium?"

"She did. What do you want to know?"

"Why don't you start with Abram Davids?"

"Why don't I start with breakfast and you can ask as I go along?"

I poured a cup of coffee and sat down at the table. Ruth meanwhile got busy cracking eggs. "How does an omelet sound?" she asked.

"Fine. As long as I can put ketchup on it."

"You always did before. What's to stop you now?" She took out the egg beater and worked the eggs over. "Where were we?"

"Abram Davids."

She stopped beating for the moment as she thought about it. "He's somewhere in his early sixties. Sixty, I think. Or is it sixty-one? Wait a minute. I've got it written down somewhere." She left and returned a couple of minutes later. "Sixty-one. What else do you want to know?"

"Where did he come from?"

"Back east. The Boston area. He's a graduate of Boston University with a Ph.D. in psychology. He came right out of school to Woodhollow in 1947. Ada says the director, who was about to retire, was an old friend of the family. Davids assisted for a few years, then was put in charge. He was in charge until Woodhollow closed a few years ago.

"Then it has closed for good?"

"As far as Ada knows."

"What about Davids' reputation?"

"No black eyes, if that's what you're looking for.

179

Though Ada says he was a better administrator than doctor, whatever that means."

"It means he's found his niche: comfortable mediocrity."

"More power to him then."

"What about Woodhollow? What did Cousin Ada have to say about it?"

"It was once a going concern. The Colburn area held its own up until the early sixties. Then it began to lose ground. You know what it's like now. You'd have to pay a rat to live there. That was bound to affect Woodhollow, and it did. Most of the patients, what there were of them, had been there for a long time. When they died, so did Woodhollow."

Still Davids could afford a Mercedes. I had to wonder.

"Thanks, Ruth. What about Aunt Emma and Wilmer?"

"She's going to call me sometime today. I told her before six."

"Why before six?"

She got busy beating eggs. "I figured you'd want to know as soon as possible."

I doubted that was the reason, but I let it pass.

At one minute after nine I called Rupert. He must've been sitting by the phone. He answered on the first ring.

"I told Elvira it was you," he said.

"Who else? Do you have any answers for me?"

"Not many. I called Woodhollow, but couldn't raise anybody. I made some other calls and didn't have any luck there. Finally Elvira said she knew someone that might help me out. A friend of hers in Phillips was a nurse there for a few years before she moved north. The long and short of it is that you were right about Nellie being in Woodhollow twice. She was admitted the first time in 1947 or 1948, somewhere in there." He paused. I heard Elvira in the background. "Elvira says it was the summer of 1947. She and Gertie arrived about the same time."

"Gertie?"

"Elvira's friend. Anyway, the second time was in the early 1950s. Gertie's less sure of that date."

"Who admitted her? Does she remember that?"

"As far as she knows, Nellie admitted herself."

"Does she know if Nellie's still there?"

"No. She left soon after Nellie came the second time."

"Did she offer an opinion about Dr. Davids, the man who used to run the place?"

"Hold on. I'll ask Elvira." I waited while he did. "No opinion. She didn't know you wanted one." I thought I heard him chewing on something. "Anything else? My breakfast is getting cold."

"This is about Woodhollow. Was there ever any kind of trouble there?"

"What kind of trouble?"

"Your kind of trouble?"

"No. Not that I remember."

"Thanks, Rupert."

I hung up. As I did, I heard Ruth pattering across the living room again. This would be as good a time as any to make my exit. In doing so, I nearly ran over Deputy Harold Clark, who'd come for Big-Ears' bones. I opened Jessie's trunk and handed them to him. He looked less than pleased with the exchange.

I got in Jessie and drove southwest toward Colburn. After a quiet night the wind had started to blow again, bringing with it long strands of cirrus that soon stretched across the sky, striping it blue and white. I passed an acre of pumpkins, a wagon of corn, and a field of turkeys. I watched as the wind scooped an armful of leaves and hurled them against a fence, where they fluttered momentarily, then dropped to the ground. I rolled down my window and stuck out my head and took one long draft of fall. It tasted good to me.

After several stops at empty houses and a conference with one old man who scratched his beard, shook his head, and replied, "You can't get there from here," I finally found Woodhollow Sanitarium.

Located four miles from Colburn along a forever winding road that crossed itself in three different places, Woodhollow sat right in the middle of a hardwood grove with no neighbors in sight. Its buildings, which were Georgian brick and looked like transplants from the antebellum South, sat on a rise at the edge of a hollow, while the grounds lay in the hollow itself. All was surrounded by a black wrought-iron fence about six feet high.

I stopped at the gate. It was closed and locked. I took a moment to look around. Ruth was right. Woodhollow looked more like a rich man's estate than anything else, a far cry from the concentration camp I had pictured in my mind. True, there was a fence around it and the gate was locked, but that was the extent of it. There was no barbed wire, no guards in towers brandishing submachine guns, no killer watchdogs patrolling the grounds. The most menacing thing around was a small white poodle that had slipped through the gate and was sniffing Jessie's tires, doing a joyful little dance as he did.

I saw a small Mexican in a white shirt coming toward me. He carried a rake in his right hand and what appeared to be a chip on his shoulder. I knew now I'd come to the right place.

He stopped at the gate and peered through its bars at me. "What do you want?" he asked.

"I came to see Abram Davids."

"What about?"

"That's between him and me."

He shrugged. He was on the inside. I was on the outside looking in. If I didn't want to tell him, that was fine with him. He'd just go back to raking leaves and I'd go back to wherever I came from.

"Okay, tell him I came to see Nellie Brainard. I heard she was a patient here."

He shook his head, looking certain. "No patients here. Last one died five, six years ago."

"Funny, Woody told me she was here."

"Woody?"

"Woody Padgett. Tall and thin guy. Big on heart, not too long on brains. Drives a red Ford pickup. He and Nellie are old friends." Then I showed him the badge I carried in my wallet for such emergencies. It was a special deputy's badge that Rupert had given me two years ago when we were both three sheets to the wind. It looked more official than it really was.

"I'll go get my boss," he said, suddenly nervous.

"I was hoping you would."

Dr. Abram Davids appeared with the Mexican a few minutes later. He was still bald, his ears still small and red, and he still looked like a walrus to me. But he was neither as fat nor as soft as he seemed. I remembered that from our first meeting. But I'd forgotten when talking to Wilmer and listening to his description of Davids as the "fat man."

"So we meet again," he said. He was polite, though not cordial, and more relaxed than the first time I saw him.

"It appears we do."

"May I see your badge, please?"

I showed it to him.

"It says you're a *special* deputy. From my understanding those are a dime a dozen."

"I can come back with a plain old ordinary one if you like. Or a sheriff, if you want to go all the way to the top."

He backed off a little. "What is it you want here?"

"To see Nellie Brainard."

"Why?"

"That's between her and me."

"She's not here."

"Then I'll wait until she gets back."

"Who says she's coming back?"

I shrugged. "Where else is she going to go?"

I never knew why, but Davids nodded to the Mexican who opened the gate and let me in. Then Davids got in Jessie and told me where to go. I parked Jessie beside his Mercedes, and we got out.

"Why don't I show you around while you're waiting?" he suggested. "Perhaps I can answer any questions you might have about Nellie."

I thought it over. He seemed affable enough. For now I'd play his game. "Fine. Where do we start?"

"Follow me."

He took me inside what was once the sanitarium. It was all one building with several adjoining wings that met in the center like spokes of a wheel. Built sometime in the middle 1800s, it had started as a farm house, Davids told me, and didn't become a sanitarium until 1920. For only the rich, he pointed out, until the Depression, and then a lot of the newly rich became the newly poor. Then the doors opened a little wider, and it became more of a hospital, less of a resort. They'd even taken out the steam baths and the tennis courts, though that was before his time.

"When was your time?" I asked.

"I came here in 1947," he answered. "As you can see, I'm still here."

"Are you still practicing?"

"No. We closed down five years ago. Once the area started to deteriorate, it was only a matter of time. Help and other services were too hard to find. Meanwhile costs were going up every year. The same old story."

"Still you've done well," I said.

"How's that?"

"You drive a Mercedes," I pointed out.

He shrugged. "I invested wisely."

We stopped at the end of a long wing. I could hear the wind whistle along the eaves, the way it did at Grandmother Ryland's when I'd lie in bed with owl eyes and a full bladder, afraid to put one bare foot on that cold dark

184

floor. Sprinkles of sunlight slipped under a door and dusted the hall at my feet, but were swept away by a passing cloud.

"What do you think of the place?" Davids asked.

"I think you need more light."

"I never noticed." He started back the other way. I followed.

"How did you happen to get interested in Nellie Brainard?" he asked.

"Through Woody Padgett," I answered.

"Describe him for me."

I described Woody as best I could.

"Yes. I remember him. He used to visit Nellie quite regularly."

"Used to?"

"We've been closed for five years."

"Then what's Nellie still doing here?"

He stopped to look at me. Though he smiled, his eyes didn't. They were grey and cold, December eyes. "She's a special case."

"In what way special?"

"She's my wife."

I looked at him. His face said he wasn't lying. "Since when?" I asked.

"A long time" was his answer.

We came to the lobby, or what used to be the lobby. "Seen enough?" he asked.

"I think so."

"Then I'll show you the grounds."

We went outside and began walking the grounds, as the brisk south wind pelted us with falling leaves and brought us a warm earthy scent from somewhere deep in the woods. I guessed there were nearly twenty acres enclosed here—a choice piece of property, even for Wisconsin.

"You've answered some of my questions," I said. "And raised others."

"Such as?"

"Why did Nellie come back here the second time?"

"That's easy enough. She liked it here."

"Then why did she leave in the first place?"

That was harder to answer. He took a moment to think about it. "Her parents wanted her home."

"After she tried to stick a meat fork through her mother?"

"That was nearly a year before. Nellie had changed since then. She'd stopped confusing her inner world with reality, blaming her parents for all of her pain."

"Are you saying you cured her in a year? That's fast, even for Woodhollow."

He smiled again, though again his eyes didn't. "You cure a ham, or a side of bacon. With someone like Nellie you teach control and balance, how to function in the real world."

"Which is why she readmitted herself to Woodhollow a few short years later?"

He didn't smile at that, nor did he attempt an answer.

We'd reached the end of the grounds and were now looking through the wrought iron fence at a deep ravine leading away from the hollow. Davids looked larger, more threatening than he had inside. Maybe because I was so far from help.

"You did know that Nellie's parents died within days of her release from Woodhollow?" I asked. "Under less than normal circumstances?"

Something flickered in his eyes, as he looked past me, through the fence at the gulley beyond. It seemed at that moment he wanted to throw both of us over the edge. "I know," he answered.

"And that Nellie's first husband drove off one day and was never seen again, leaving a fortune behind?"

He doubled his hands into fists, then opened them again. I noted the hands. They were large, meaty, powerful. I wouldn't want them around my throat.

186

"I know all that. What does that have to do with me?"

"I just wondered. You say you and Nellie are married. If so, why did you marry her? Was it for love . . . or for some other reason?"

"It was for love," a woman's voice interrupted.

I spun around to see Nellie Brainard standing less than ten feet away.

19

"**Nellie, I told you** I'd handle this," Davids said.

"And I told you I could fight my own battles."

They faced each other uncertainly, like two boxers feeling each other out, each afraid to throw his best Sunday punch for fear he'd see the other still standing. Davids was the first to lower his guard. For now he'd settle for a draw—if she would.

"Do as you please," he said. "You always have."

"I please," she answered. There was an edge of steel in her soft voice.

He turned abruptly and started the long walk back the way we'd come. For a big man he was unusually light on his feet and moved with grace and power not unlike that of a grizzly. I wasn't sorry to see him go.

"So, Mr. Ryland, what do you want with me?"

I studied her. She hadn't changed much over the years. There were streaks of grey in her short dark hair, only a trace of wear on her otherwise flawless face. Her breasts were still firm, her body trim and supple. She looked about forty-five, though I knew she was at least ten years past that. And her eyes were those of a child, dark blue and clear and curious to the extreme. In spite of what I knew about her, I found myself awed by her. In person she was even more beautiful than her portrait.

"How did you know my name?" I asked.

She laughed at that. "Come on, Mr. Ryland. We're not that far out in the sticks. We sometimes even buy a newspaper, yours included. I remember you from your picture."

"I'm flattered." Though I doubted that was how she knew me.

"So am I . . . by all of the attention you seem to be showing me. I wondered what I did to deserve all of it."

The question seemed innocent enough, but I had to wonder. Nellie was a charmer. I wondered if she was working her spell on me. If so, she knew how to make the knife seem painless.

"I didn't start with you," I said. "I started with Woody Padgett. He disappeared from Oakalla two weeks ago tomorrow. In looking for him, I discovered you."

"What did you discover?" Her smile was direct, playful, much like Diana's. I liked her smile.

"I discovered your past."

"What about my past? Did you discover I attacked my mother with a meat fork, that I in fact tried to kill her, would have if my father hadn't interfered? Did you also discover that I was seventeen at the time and had spent the last month locked in my room, was beaten almost daily with a razor strap? That I shed no tears when my parents died and would have danced on their grave had I been permitted?"

"Who was to stop you?"

"I was," she answered, no longer smiling. "That part

189

of me that realized my parents, my foster parents really, my fourth set of them, were decent but misguided souls who never should have been given a child in the first place. If God in his infinite wisdom saw fit not to give them one, why then did the state of Wisconsin? They would have been better served with a robot, something that had no will of its own."

"Still you went home to them after you left Wood-hollow. Why?" I wanted to know.

She sighed. "Where else was I to go? Woodhollow released me into their care. I could either go home or run away. I chose not to run away. It seemed I'd been running from something or someone all my life. It was time to make my stand."

"By killing your parents?"

The question should have surprised her. It didn't. "Who told you that?"

"I heard rumors."

"That's all they are, rumors. I was home in bed with the mumps when my parents died. I was too sick even to attend the funeral. Ask anyone in Oakalla."

"I asked Wilmer Wiemer. He told me you once asked him to help you kill your parents."

She gave a forgiving smile. "I wouldn't believe everything Wilmer tells you. I know I never did."

"And Wilmer was never your lover?"

"Of course, he was! At a very early age. Wilmer, at one time or another, was almost everyone's lover. He was quite the ladies' man. I know I was quite taken with him."

"What about Big-Ears Brainard? Was he quite the ladies' man?"

Her face darkened as her eyes caught fire. I'd touched the rawest of nerves. "Calvin Brainard was a tyrant, the most ruthless, egotistical man I've ever met. He liked inflicting pain on people. It gave him great pleasure."

"Still you married him. Why?"

190

"I was adrift, that's why. My parents had just died. I had no family, no friends to speak of. I was alone in the world. Again. For the hundredth time it seemed. Calvin Brainard had money and property and a place in the community, all the things I'd wanted, yet never had. Marrying him seemed the answer to everything." Her eyes clouded. She seemed to shrink, become small and child-like. "In truth it was the answer to nothing."

"And *power*," I reminded her. "That's another name for money and property and prestige."

"Of course, power," she said. "When you're orphaned and alone, you're drawn to power like a moth to light. At least I was. You haven't learned yet how it can be abused, used against you to hammer you into place, then nail your feet to the floor to keep you there."

"Except you didn't stay nailed to the floor."

She smiled. It was a grim, triumphant smile, a soldier's battle smile. "No. I didn't."

"You killed him and took his money."

She turned her smile on me. Then she laughed in my face. "Is that what you think? Then I've misjudged you all along. I thought you were smarter than that."

"Tell me where I'm wrong."

"The money for one thing. If I had it, what would I still be doing here?"

"I have a reason, but I'll pass on that."

"And if I killed him, why wasn't his body ever found?"

"Rumor has it, it was."

"When?" Her voice sharpened, sprang out at me.

"Recently."

"Why didn't anyone tell me?"

"I just did."

It was her turn to study me. As she did, she slowly relaxed, became mellow again. But I felt I'd caught a glimpse of the real Nellie, seen the claws exposed, then withdrawn. It made me uneasy, like canoeing a strange

191

river for the first time. Though the waters appeared calm, you never knew what might be around the next bend. Especially when you'd heard there was white water ahead.

"You're not quite what you seem," she said.

"Either one of us."

Her eyes shifted from me to survey the rest of Woodhollow. She appeared to be searching for Davids, but he was nowhere in sight. I was just as glad he wasn't.

"You mentioned Woody Padgett," she said, "that he was missing. How did Woody lead you to me?"

"You and Woody are old friends. He's been looking after the Brainard estate for you. He's been known to visit you here. I thought you might have seen him lately."

"No. Not for the past ten years."

"That long ago? Your husband said only five."

"Then he's mistaken." The claws were inching out again, as she again surveyed the grounds. It was time I left. I'd almost worn out my welcome.

"For love, you said."

"What was that?" Her gaze turned to me.

"Abram Davids married you for love. Why did you marry him?"

Her eyes bore into mine with white heat. I had to look away. "I didn't marry him. I married Woodhollow."

"I don't suppose you care to explain that?"

"No. I don't."

I started walking back to where Jessie was parked. I stopped once for a last look at Nellie. There was a fierce look on her face, like that of our first meeting some thirty years before. I felt the hairs on the back of my neck stand straight out. It was all I could do to keep from running.

I got in Jessie and prayed she'd start. She did. I drove to the gate. The Mexican was waiting for me there. He still carried the rake in his right hand and a set of keys in the other. But I noticed he now wore a pistol on his belt. I didn't remember seeing one there before.

192

On my way out the drive I saw Nellie striding rapidly across the grounds of Woodhollow, the poodle I'd seen earlier following her like a small white shadow, dancing as he did. It should have been comical to watch, brought a smile to even the most hardened heart. But I shuddered and gave thanks that I was back on the outside looking in.

20

I should have gone home. I didn't. I drove a half mile down the road, found a place to turn around, and backed Jessie into it. I didn't have long to wait. Before I even saw it coming, the red pickup was on me and past.

I pulled out onto the road and started to follow it. Two could play this game. We went almost a mile before the driver of the pickup noticed I was back there. He'd been racing along, checking every turn and crossroad to see which way I'd gone, and was much too busy to look in his rear-view mirror. When he finally did, I came as a real surprise to him.

He gradually increased his speed. So did I. He slowed down. I did the same, keeping a safe distance behind him. I wanted to find out who was driving the pickup, but I didn't want to end up wearing it.

He gradually increased his speed again, continuing to accelerate down a long steep hill. I followed the leader, but when the speedometer hit seventy, I quit looking. At seventy-five Jessie would start to shimmy. At eighty she'd self destruct.

We roared down to the bottom, shot up the next small hill, and popped over the top, where my head hit the roof and my stomach left for parts unknown. Meanwhile the pickup continued to pull away from me. It came to a curve. I saw its brake lights go on, as it slowed momentarily, then swept on through. That looked easy enough— until my right front tire blew.

I went into the curve sideways, spun a hundred and eighty degrees, jumped a ditch, and plowed a corn field. Ears, stalks, and jimsonweed flew over my head. I closed my eyes and hung on. When I opened them again, I was back on the road, facing the way I'd come. I didn't bother to look for the pickup. It was long gone.

I got out of Jessie and stood for a moment testing my legs. Both were working, though I couldn't get them to go the same direction. When I finally did, I took a slow walk around Jessie to assess the damage.

Nothing that couldn't be fixed. Her muffler and tail pipe were gone, but I needed new ones anyway. A couple new dents, but they matched the old ones. I crawled under her to make sure the oil pan was okay. It was. It seemed all I had to do now was to change the tire, and I'd soon be on my way home.

But when I opened the trunk to remove the spare, I discovered it was flat. I also found the note Ruth had left for me. It read, "I told you to get this thing fixed." I had to smile in spite of myself. She'd made her point.

I looked up and down the road. There wasn't a house in sight. The only thing to do was to start walking.

At the first house, a mile away, no one was home. At the second house, a half mile beyond that, the only thing home was a large brown dog who looked like he hadn't eaten in a month. He stood in the yard growling at me. I stood in the road threatening him. Neither one of us had the guts to find out if the other was serious.

I looked at my watch. It was already midafternoon. At the earliest it was going to be evening before I got home. And judging by the sky, which had started to grey in the west, it was going to be an early evening at that.

By now I was out of the fields and into the woods. The road began to narrow, as the trees crowded alongside it like the stakes of a gauntlet. I came to a humped one-lane bridge that crossed over a small stream. At the same time I smelled cedar smoke. It seemed to be following the stream.

I came to a battered mailbox and two ruts leading into the woods. About an eighth of a mile in I found a small log cabin built into the side of a hill. The stream that I'd crossed wound its way past the cabin and gave it the only boundary it would ever want or need. I liked the cabin and its setting, the way it hugged the hill between the creek and woods, snug as a bug in a rug. Solitude. You could have all you ever wanted here. But I was afraid that probably along about February I'd start talking to the squirrels.

I stood and watched a wizened little man gather hickory nuts. Moving slowly and surely, he raked the leaves back with his foot, then bent over, picked up the nuts, and put them in a burlap sack. Gradually he worked his way toward me.

"Hello," I said when he was about ten feet away.

He took no notice of me.

"Hello!" I yelled, making sure he heard me.

He set the sack down and looked at me with flinty blue eyes. "I'm just old, son. Not deaf." Then he went back to gathering hickory nuts.

When he was finished, he shouldered the sack and motioned for me to follow him. We went as far as the porch of his cabin, where we sat on a huge beech slab that he'd cut and set upon two stumps. Looking at his cabin,

196

which was tight and solidly built, I knew it hadn't come in a kit.

"Nice place," I said.

"I like it."

"How long did it take you to build it?"

"About a year. Six months to cut and season the wood. Six months to put it up."

"How long have you lived here?"

"Forever. Or so it seems. But it's closer to twenty years."

"It ever get lonely out here?"

"Used to. Not so much anymore. I've sort of gotten to like the quiet."

"I don't suppose you neighbor much?"

"Can't. No neighbors. Except Wilbur. And he's dead."

I nodded. It made sense to me. "You don't happen to have any spare tires around, do you?"

"What happened? You lose yours?"

"Something like that. I had a blowout about two miles from here. When I looked in my trunk, my spare was flat."

He shook his head. "Got no extra tires. I've got a hand pump and patching material though. That might hold you until you can get back home, wherever that is."

"Oakalla. I'm Garth Ryland. I publish the *Oakalla Reporter*."

I offered my hand and he shook it. His hand was dry and rough, like his face. "Long way from home, aren't you?" he asked.

"It seems like it."

"Well, hop in the jeep and we'll see what we can do about fixing that tire of yours."

I got in his jeep, while he went inside his storage shed, looking for the pump and patching material. The jeep was an International, vintage 1950s, and looked like it had never missed a bump in its life. I sat on the edge of the seat. It was either that or sit on the spring.

He returned with a smile. He'd found everything he needed.

"Ready?" he asked.

"When you are," I answered.

I hadn't understood his question. When he asked if I were ready, I assumed it was to leave. I didn't realize it was to meet my Maker. And he drove like we were already three hours late.

I held on to everything I could, including the steering wheel. But I still bounced around like a cork in a caldron. I didn't have time to give him directions. And with both hands occupied, the best I could do was nod.

The old man seemed not to notice. And when we skidded to a stop behind Jessie, he had a look of pure serenity on his face. I guessed he'd lived too long to care how he died.

"Looks like we made it," he said.

I was untangling myself from the spring. "You couldn't prove it by me."

We got out, and I opened Jessie's trunk and took out the spare tire. Meanwhile the old man was giving Jessie the once over. "I used to know a woman that owned a car like this," he said. "But she's dead now."

"What was her name?"

"Anna Marie Ryland," he said with reverence. "Finest woman I ever knew."

"She was my grandmother."

"I thought she might be."

"How did you happen to know Grandmother?"

"I used to run the elevator there in Colburn before I shut down. She used to come in for feed every Saturday morning. Used to make my day. I could hardly wait for Friday to get over with, just so I could see her again."

"Did you ever tell her how you felt?"

He grimaced and shook his head. "No. I never had the courage. I guess in my heart I knew I wasn't good enough for her. It's just as well I suppose, her being dead

198

and all. I couldn't stand to lose a woman like that. Probably would've killed me too."

"I still think you should've told her. That way you wouldn't have any regrets." I was thinking more of myself. Maybe I'd let Diana go too easily. Maybe I should've pleaded my case more strongly.

He looked at me and smiled. "There are always regrets, son. Things you did. Things you didn't do. You can't escape them. They're bound up in life and the living of it. That's what makes it so damned interesting, knowing you can make a mess of things one moment and maybe make them right the next. The trick is not to take it all to heart. Better men than me or you have tried and failed. Lesser men have conquered, been made kings and presidents. And to know you tried ain't always enough either. We all like to catch the brass ring sometime."

"So what's the answer?" I asked.

"There ain't none," he said. "Just go on living and doing your best. And don't wait on either heaven or earth to pat you on the back. It might be a long time in coming. In heaven's case, maybe never." He went back to the jeep after the pump and patches, while I stood in the middle of the road waiting for him.

He took the tube out of the spare and pumped air into it. He clicked his tongue as he did. Then he looked at me and shook his head. He no doubt thought the Ryland line was on the descent.

Seven patches later the tube would finally hold air. We deflated it, put it in the tire, and pumped it up again. When it stayed up, I put the tire on Jessie.

"You might consider a new tire," he said, wiping his hands on his pants.

"I guess I'll have to."

"Five of them in fact. The last tires I saw like those were on a tugboat."

I nodded. "Thanks for your help."

He picked a corn husk from Jessie's windshield. "And it might help if you stay on the road."

"I plan to from now on."

"If you drove like me, these things wouldn't happen."

"If I drove like you, I'd need landing gear."

He smiled. "You've got some of your grandmother in you all right."

"I take that as a compliment."

"You should."

I kept waiting for him to leave. When he didn't, I asked, "Was there something else?"

"I just wondered what you were chasing or what was chasing you."

"A red pickup. You haven't seen it around, have you?"

"As a matter of fact I have. A couple of times. Burning up the road each time."

"Did you see who was driving it?"

"Once I did. That'd be Monday a week. It came by my place like a bat, went over that humped bridge like it wasn't there, and landed somewhere toward the end of the road. That crossroad ain't marked. I figured there was no way it'd make the turn. I was right. It didn't."

"What time was that?"

"After midnight. I'd say along about one or two. I'd just got back from visiting a lady friend."

"And you saw who was driving it?"

"I'm getting to that. I got in my jeep and went down there. By then it'd nearly got itself out of the pasture, but it had to make a circle to do it. It came right out of the pasture into my bright lights. I saw the driver. I couldn't see who was on the other side—or if there was anybody at all."

"What did the driver look like? Do you remember?"

"Mad. She had a scowl on her face that would've turned a lesser man to salt."

"*She?* The driver was a woman?"

"I thought that's what I said."

"You couldn't be mistaken?"

"Son, I've been out in these sticks a long time, but I still know a woman when I see one."

"Do you remember anything else about her?"

"Nope. Just that she was mad at the world. She damn near ran over me getting out of there."

"Thanks . . ." I was embarrassed. I didn't even know his name.

"Harry," he said. "Harry Thompson."

"I'll remember."

21

I got in Jessie and drove back to Oakalla. It was dusk when I got to Woody's, the same time it was nearly two weeks before when Woody disappeared. Two weeks? It seemed more like two years.

As I climbed out of Jessie, I was hit by a gust of wind that raked the woods and swept on down the hill toward Stony Creek. It had a bite to it and smelled of rain.

I searched the house first. I didn't expect to find Woody here, but it was at least worth one more look. I used a screwdriver to pry at the floorboards, looking for a loose one. I found none. I lay flat on the floor and smelled between the cracks. I smelled nothing dead.

I took the flashlight from Jessie's glove compartment and searched the area around the barn. I'd done this before in daylight and found nothing, but sometimes the subtle shades of night were best for finding those things hidden by day. Contrasts were especially revealing. With less to see, you focused on what you could see. Nevertheless, I didn't find Woody.

I went inside the barn and turned on the light. The wind hit a temporary lull and all was quiet in here, except for a couple sparrows fluttering nervously on their perch. I climbed into the mow and began restacking bales of hay, working my way toward the bottom of the mow. There was always the chance that Woody was in here. But he wasn't.

I climbed down from the mow and stood staring at the shovel with the dirt on it. If it hadn't been used to bury Woody, what then had it been used for? I thought at last I knew. I also thought I knew where Woody had gone and why. And for the first time in several days I had the faint hope he might still be alive.

Thelma Osterday sat on her back stoop hulling walnuts. I put on a pair of gloves and helped her. We worked in silence for a while, as she sorted her thoughts. I noticed the wind was still blowing. It was going to be another restless night.

"How much do you know?" she finally asked.

"Not much. But I have a lot of guesses you can help me with."

"Why should I?"

"Because Woody's life depends on it."

"How do you know he's not already dead?"

"I don't. But the odds are still in his favor. They won't be for much longer though. It's up to you. The way I see it, his life is now in your hands."

"Then you don't know Woody very well."

"I'm learning that."

She sighed in resignation. "But I've let it go too long already. So go ahead. Guess."

"Okay, my first guess is that Woody found the money in the Cadillac and buried it. That's how the dirt got on the shovel."

"What shovel?"

"Never mind. Am I right? Did Woody find the money?"

"Yes. Woody found the money."

"And hid it?"

"Yes. He hid it. Though he didn't tell me where."

"And he told you this when he brought the Snickers and Cokes here?"

"Yes. Yes! Yes! And Yes! Get on with it, will you?"

"Details are important, Thelma. They might not be to you, but they are to me. I think I know where Woody is, but I'm not sure. Every detail helps tell me whether I'm right or wrong."

"I'm sorry, Garth. I'm just sick with worry, that's all. Woody was supposed to be back here that next morning bright and early. But he didn't show up and I haven't heard a word from him since. . . ." She started to cry, but caught herself. "No!" she said, wiping her eye with her sleeve. "I won't let myself do that!"

"It might help."

"The only thing that will help is for Woody to come back safe and sound." She grabbed two handfuls of walnuts and threw them down in anger. "I told him it wouldn't work! I told him!"

I began retrieving the walnuts. I hated to work for nothing. "What wouldn't work?"

"The whole thing. From the beginning."

"From the time I found the car?"

"From the time he went to work for Nellie Brainard thirty-five years ago. Woody wasn't as dumb as everybody thought he was. Innocent maybe—there wasn't a mean bone in his body—but not dumb. When he heard about Big-Ears Brainard's missing money, he figured out a way to get close to it. He went right to the source."

"Who was Nellie?"

"Right. Who was Nellie. He had an agreement with her. He'd look after her place for her and help her look for the money, providing she'd go half with him when they found it."

"And Nellie agreed to that?"

"She agreed to it. But I knew she'd never keep her word. I told Woody as much. He didn't agree with me. He said he thought she'd play it straight, that half a loaf was better than none."

"Did he ever change his mind?"

"Not that I know of. Woody had a thing about loyalty. He didn't know how to be anything else. Besides, he figured he'd find it first, take out his share, then give her the rest. That way, he said, I could have all the things I'd always wanted."

"He was doing it for you?"

She gave me her first smile of the evening. "Don't look so surprised. At one time I was a handsome woman. More woman than Nellie Brainard could ever hope to be. Yes, Woody was doing it for me. Though I never asked him to."

"Then why did you marry someone else?"

"Because I was a fool. We all are when we're young. Some of us are just luckier than others. We somehow stay single. Or stumble into marrying the right person."

I couldn't argue with that. "So after Nellie left, Woody stayed on, protecting his interest in the money?"

"That and the fact he liked the place. He didn't want to see it fall to rack and ruin."

"Did Nellie ever tell Woody why she was leaving?"

"She hated the place. Had from the moment she first set foot on it. The only reason she stayed was because of the money. But after a time even that wasn't enough to keep her there."

"And the reason she went back to Woodhollow?"

"She knew they'd take care of her there, that once she knocked on the door, they'd have to let her in."

"She went home," I said.

"How do you figure?"

"There's a line of poetry. It was spoken by the

husband in Frost's *The Death of the Hired Man*. 'Home is the place where, when you have to go there, They have to take you in.'"

"Sounds sort of hard-hearted to me."

"It is." But in Nellie's case, appropriate. "Tell me this, Thelma, when Woody was looking after the Brainard place, why did he always work at night?"

"He didn't. Not always. Only when he couldn't get to it in the daytime." She smiled again. She was proud of Woody. "And there was one advantage to working at night."

"The ghost of Big-Ears Brainard?"

"It *did* keep the others away and made Woody's work a lot easier."

"I imagine it did." I could see Woody now, smiling to himself as he hammered away. "And, of course, you never said differently."

Though the smile was still on her face, I thought I saw a tear shining in her eye. "Never. We had a lot of fun over that, Woody and I."

"Maybe it's not all in the past."

"I hope not, Garth. I truly do. All that money aside."

"What did you plan to do with it, anyway?"

"See the world. At least as much of it as we wanted. After that we thought we'd settle down in California. Try life in the fast lane for a while."

"You aren't happy here?"

"Sure. Happy enough, I guess. But hell, maybe it's because I don't know any better, having never lived anywhere else."

"I have. I like Oakalla."

"I haven't. I'm not so sure."

I took off my gloves. It was about time to leave. "Wilmer told me he really did run across Big-Ears Brainard one night. Ruth also said something to that effect, that there were a lot of holes dug that people couldn't explain.

Was Woody the one digging those holes or was it someone else?"

"Someone else."

"Do you know who he was?"

"No. Woody caught him digging one night and asked what he was doing. He was drunk, Woody said. He asked Woody who in the hell wanted to know. Then before Woody could answer, he said no chicken-shit handyman was going to run him off his own place. That Woody had better get out of there if he knew what was good for him."

"What did Woody say to that?"

"He held his ground. He said if the man didn't leave, he'd call the sheriff on him for trespassing. At that the man threw his shovel at Woody, intending to hurt him. But he missed. Woody picked up the shovel and just walked away."

"Do you remember when this was?"

"A long time ago. It was sometime after Nellie left for Woodhollow."

"Do you mind if we back up a step?"

"No. Forward or back, it's all the same to me. As long as it'll help get Woody back."

"That Tuesday morning I stopped by here on my way to the Brainard mansion, you muttered something about your missing comforter. 'It isn't possible,' I think you said."

"'It ain't possible' is what I said."

"What did you mean by that?"

"Nellie Brainard. I couldn't believe it was her, not after all the years."

"But did you actually see her?"

"Nope. Though Liddy Bennett swore she did. Of course, Liddy swore she saw a flying saucer month before last. I wouldn't borrow money to bet on anything she says."

"I just wondered. I found Liddy's bread and milk at the Brainard mansion too."

"It does make you wonder, doesn't it?"

"One last question to remember me by?"

"You don't have to make it so final. But go ahead. Fire away."

"Where did Woody go after he left here? Was it to see Nellie to tell her about the money?"

"It might've been. That's my best guess."

"Mine too."

"But how can we know for sure?"

I thought a moment, back to the first day I searched Woody's house. I remembered something that I'd forgotten, that I never should have forgotten. "Hang on to your hopes, Thelma. I just might have the answer to that question."

I drove home, went to my closet, and found the shirt I was looking for. It was the same shirt I'd worn when I searched Woody's house for the first time. I took the worn piece of paper out of the pocket and dialed the number written there. I waited through seven rings. I was about to hang up when I heard someone answer. "Hello. Abram Davids speaking."

I smiled grimly and hung up.

I called Rupert. No one was home at his house. I called the dispatcher at the sheriff's office. She didn't know where Rupert was. He was off duty today and planned to stay that way. I told her to have him call me if he called in.

I thought about going to the Woodhollow Sanitarium alone, but decided against it. The odds were at least two to one and not in my favor. I wasn't afraid of the Mexican guard nearly as much as I was of Dr. Abram Davids. For a big man he had very quick and quiet feet. He could be on you before you knew it, and after that it was Katie bar the door. And there was one more possibility—one that frightened me most of all.

I walked to the window and looked out. I saw Liddy Bennet drive by in her purple station wagon. It looked like Ruth sandwiched in the middle between Liddy and Wanda Collum.

Ruth! What in the hell was she doing out and about?

Her bedroom door was closed. I had thought she was upstairs taking her Sunday nap.

Then it all came back to me—how she'd been given just three days to make up her missed Thursday night bowl, how I'd caught her shadow-bowling in the living room this morning. No wonder her face turned red. I'd caught her in the act and didn't know it. I'd been too busy with my own schemes to think about hers.

I went into the kitchen. Maybe she'd left me a note. She usually did when she felt guilty about something. I found the note on the kitchen table and read it. "Got the goods on Wilmer. Will tell you all about it when I get back. Don't worry. I'll be fine. Ruth."

I shook my head, then crumpled the note and threw it away. There was nothing I could do about it now. While she was gone, I might as well make the best of it.

I poured a beer, fixed a bowl of popcorn, and sat down in my easy chair. Sitting there in the soft light of my floor lamp, I began to nod. I let myself go, thinking I could pull out of it whenever I wanted to. I underestimated how tired I was.

22

I didn't realize how long I slept. I dreamed I heard Ruth's
Volkswagen pull up out back. But it seemed to take forever
for her to get to the door. The phone rang.

"Garth Ryland?" The voice was muffled, like he was
talking through a handkerchief.

"Yes. Who's this?"

"Never mind. We have something of yours. You have
something of ours. If you want yours back, you'll do
exactly as I say. Are you listening?"

"I'm listening." The terrible thought struck me that it
wasn't a dream after all, that there was a reason why Ruth
had never made it to the door.

"Is the Cadillac within walking distance?"

"Yes, it is."

"Good. Someone is watching you right now. You will
be followed to the Cadillac. Get in it, drive slowly to the
four-way stop, circle the block once, slowly, never stopping,

and turn past the Marathon Service Station down Fair Haven Road. Drive slowly down Fair Haven Road, past the Brainard mansion, until you come to the first crossroad. Turn your car around and wait. I'll flash my lights at you and turn into the mansion's lane. Follow me then. Drive to the mansion, as far down the lane as you can. Get out of the car and leave the keys in it. My partner will check you on this. If the keys are there, my partner will flash his light. I will be in the mansion at that point and flash a light as a signal to you. You go into the mansion by the back door. I will leave by the front door. You'll find your friend on the second floor."

"Which room?"

"You figure it out."

"How do I know my friend will still be alive?"

"You have my word on it."

"How do I know your word is any good?"

"It is. I assure you. That is why you can know that if you don't do exactly as I said, you'll never see your friend again."

"And you can know that if that happens, you'll never know a moment's peace until I see you dead."

"Fine. We understand each other. I'm hanging up now. You do the same."

I disconnected the line, but I didn't put down the receiver. I chanced a quick call to Rupert. I waited three rings. When no one answered, I hung up. For Ruth's sake I couldn't afford to wait any longer.

I went outside where the wind blew hard from the south, the leaves swirled in brown eddies, and the clouds had all but covered the moon. It was a skittish night, one that came at me from all sides with a panoply of shapes and sounds that danced past and were gone, swallowed by the wind. Jack-o'-lanterns grinned at me through crooked teeth and tree limbs waved their shadows in my face. A dog barked. A cat hissed. Someone came to his bay window and became a black silhouette through a yellow curtain. I had the streets of Oakalla to myself.

Almost to myself. Somewhere behind me someone was following me. I glanced over my shoulder a couple times but saw nothing. Still I knew in my bones someone was there.

I walked to the City Building and threw open the overhead door. Sitting there, dusted blue by the security light outside, the Cadillac never looked better. I patted it once before I climbed inside. I doubted it would ever look so good to me again.

Following my instructions to the letter, I drove slowly to the four-way stop, circled the block, and passed the Marathon on my way north along Fair Haven Road. At that point a pickup started following me. I guessed it was Woody's. And I guessed Dr. Abram Davids was behind the wheel.

I drove to the first crossroad, turned around, and waited for my signal. It wasn't long in coming. Too soon for me to even think of doing anything else.

I drove to the Brainard estate and parked. Several yards ahead I saw the pickup. It started to bother me. Why did they bring the pickup and *not* the Mercedes if the Cadillac was all they were after? To throw me off in case I saw the Mercedes? That was one explanation. But it didn't hold up. They could just as easily have hidden the Mercedes where I couldn't see it. The Mercedes was black. The night was dark. It wouldn't be hard to do.

This thought gave rise to interesting questions: What if they had a specific reason for bringing the pickup? What if they intended to leave it here and take the Cadillac home? What if they intended to leave Ruth and me here with the pickup, implicating Woody? By the time Rupert investigated, they'd be long gone from here, and if we were dead, it wouldn't really matter to us whether they took Big-Ears' fortune or not.

I got out of the Cadillac and moved a short distance

away from it, gradually increasing the distance until I melted into a shadow. I wanted to wait to see what would happen next.

I crouched down and got my bearings. It was dark inside the mansion—dark and still, the only sounds coming from the corn field behind me, as the wind raced up and down the rows, rattling the stalks like bursts of rain and walking fingers up and down my spine. I didn't like this. Not at all. I felt like a cricket sitting here in the grass, nervously waiting for somebody to step on me.

I changed positions. I glanced at the mansion, then the Cadillac. I'd seen no one so far. And as the moon dimmed and it grew harder and harder to see, I had to squint just to stay even. My eyes began to blur, then burn. I blinked trying to get the tears to flow. But the wind dried them as fast as the tears formed. I rubbed them, thinking that would help, but it just made them feel like sandpaper.

I closed my eyes and got lost for a moment. I could smell the nearby apples fermenting, a light heady scent that brought back a bushelful of memories—of apples I'd thrown and apples I'd picked and apples I'd eaten on the steps of Grandmother Ryland's cellar. I remembered cider and pumpkin pie, how good they tasted just before bedtime as I sat in Grandmother's kitchen with my bare feet pointed toward the wood range. How long ago was that?

I glanced back at the mansion. Still dark, still no one moving inside or out. If the pickup wasn't here, I'd have to wonder what I was doing here. But it didn't drive here by itself. That meant somebody was about and being just as patient as I was.

A wild gust of wind raked the corn field and showered me with husks, as the moon momentarily peeped through the clouds, giving me a glimpse of the yard. Silver in the moonlight and slightly out of focus, the yard flickered to life, like the opening reel of an old film. I tried to see it all at once, to catch every detail, but that was like trying to catch a pumpful of water in my hands. By the time I began to sort things out, the moon went under again, and I was left wondering just what I'd seen.

Nothing for certain. The outline of a large man's body. Perhaps the pale oval of his face. And he looked burdened, like he was carrying something.

I heard something coming through the corn field toward me. I rose to a crouch and waited, wishing I had something in my hands. I tested my legs. There was still some spring in them, enough for one short charge. The stalks parted at the edge of the field, and I saw the deer at the same time he saw me. It was a buck, one of the largest I'd ever seen, with a rack of at least six points on each side. He stood there with his head raised and stock-still, aware of a danger yet undefined, but too proud to run at nothing.

He snorted at me. I hoped he wasn't out to settle an old grudge. With that rack of his he could let the air out of me in a hurry. He took a cautious step my way. Then the wind brought us both a whiff of gasoline. The buck snorted again and turned tail. The last I saw of him, he was heading east down the corn field.

I turned back to the mansion just in time to see a flashlight go on and off upstairs. I watched and waited. A few seconds later I saw a light blink on and off in the lane. That was the wrong order. But it was time I made my move.

I crossed the yard and stopped at the back door of the mansion. It was a heavy oak door with a curved brass handle and a brass tongue above it that tripped a lever inside. The door swung out at me. I went in, making sure the door stayed open.

I stood in the threshold a moment, listening for sounds. I thought I heard the front door open and softly close. Maybe I was too quick to judge. Maybe they were playing it straight after all. But somehow I doubted it.

I smelled gasoline again. Only this time it was stronger. I heard the floor creak somewhere above me. Nellie's bedroom perhaps?

Using what light I had, I eased my way through the kitchen and the dining room and onto the rosewood stairs. I was part way up the stairs when I heard the back door slam closed, shaking the mansion as it did. I hoped it was the wind, prayed it was the wind. Otherwise I might be a dead duck.

I stopped at the top of the stairs, took a deep breath, and tried to calm myself. Up here the wind roared, as it slammed into the mansion, shaking the walls and sending tremors along every floorboard. I looked down the hall in both directions. I saw no one. I started toward Nellie's room. As I did, I thought about what might be waiting there and felt my heart's drumming grow louder. Coward, it seemed to say to me. Admit it and run. And I would have, if it hadn't been for Ruth.

I stopped at the bathroom long enough to make sure no one was there, then continued on to Nellie's room. I stopped at the door. Even now I couldn't make myself go inside. Death, in one form or another, was inside. Along with the bed. It was a hard combination to face.

I closed my eyes, prayed for strength, and went in fast. I didn't want to get tagged from behind. Someone was on the bed. I could see an arm dangling down at the side. I approached it cautiously, making sure it wasn't a trap. Looking down at the one lying there, I almost cried out loud in relief. It was Woody, not Ruth, and though battered and bruised, he was still alive. Barely it seemed, though his pulse was strong.

I glanced at my watch, thinking it had stopped. It hadn't. It was only ten-thirty, much too early for Ruth to be home from bowling. A dream, plus a load of guilt had put me at death's door. Now I had to make sure it didn't close on me.

There was no time to check Woody's injuries. I threw

him over my shoulder and started out the door. Too late I heard the floorboard creak behind me.

He was on me before I could stop him. Woody went flying from my arms, as he struck me from the rear with a blow intended to break my neck. But his aim was slightly off and he hit mostly shoulder instead. Still a bone-jarring blow—enough to knock me to the floor.

Then he was on me with the fury of the damned, smashing my head into the floor again and again, as a white flame of pain and rage burned up my nose and into my brain. I tried to rise. He smashed me back down again. There was lead in his huge hands. Everything they hit they hurt. Then he yanked back my head and jammed a sweet-smelling rag in my face. Curtains, Garth. The rag was soaked with ether.

I held my breath, pushed up with my arms, got my legs under me, and took him piggyback into the wall. That hurt. But it hurt him too. I heard him grunt in pain.

But he wasn't finished with me yet. Like a good jockey, he kept his legs wrapped, applying pressure with his knees, while he slowly squeezed the breath out of me. I buckled under his weight and went to the floor again. He grasped my hair with one hand, while he tried to stuff the rag into my mouth with the other.

I bit him, hard enough to sever an ordinary finger, but his were thick and tough. He screamed. I feared that scream. It laid him open like a skinning knife and exposed the savage heart beneath. He lost control and hit me with everything he could—fists, feet, knees, elbows, the Washington Monument, the Collossus at Rhodes. Covering my head with my arms, I made like a turtle and took it for as long as I could. Then things became a hazy pink, followed by a murky red. I thought I was dying. I hoped I was dying. It might ease the pain.

No such luck. There was something within me, blame it on my ancestors, that wouldn't cry uncle, that finally took matters into its own hands and said enough was

216

enough. I came up flailing. I didn't care where I hit him as long as I hit him. And though I didn't hit him often, my arms never stopped, as I drove him away from me and part-way down the stairs. I didn't try to follow. I sank to the floor and tried to stay conscious.

But I didn't get long to rest. It seemed only an instant from the time I hit the floor until I smelled the gasoline—a river of it. Less than an instant until the whole bottom floor seemed to burst into flames. It took Davids by surprise too. He'd started back up the stairs. He didn't get far before he turned and fled.

I looked for Woody, saw him lying in the hall behind me. I crawled to him and bent over him, trying to lift him onto my shoulder, as I had before. But my arms had gone dead. It seemed so had my brain. I just knelt there, helplessly staring at him, wanting to cry. Damn it, Woody! Show me some life! Show me you're at least worth the effort!

He didn't move. I burrowed under him like a mole and somehow got him onto my shoulder. But when I tried to stand, my knees buckled and I almost fell under his weight. Staggering along the hallway, using the wall for support, I finally came to the top of the stairs. No reason to stare at shadows now. The fire gave me all the light I needed.

It had spread across the dining room and was now licking at the bottom of the stairs. The only way out was the way I had come in, and even at that I'd have to do some high stepping. Crazy. I'd only been this tired once before—in football during double sessions. So damned tired my helmet and pads felt like a suit of armor. And then I had to high step my way through the tires while someone threw dummies at my feet. It seemed impossible then.

But I gave it my best shot. I came down the stairs on the run and didn't slow down when I hit the dining room floor. Instead, I chopped even harder, hoping my momentum would carry me into the kitchen. It did, as I banged through the doorway and slammed into a wall. Resting a moment while letting the stars float away, I checked my charge. Still alive—but not conscious.

I stumbled through the kitchen and found the back door. It was locked. It wouldn't budge, not even after I nearly broke my shoulder butting it.

I grabbed Woody and half-dragged, half-carried him down the basement stairs. That was the only way left to us. No window was in sight, and the fire ruled everywhere else.

I rested at the bottom of the stairs. It was dark down here, dark and cool, but it wouldn't be for long. I tried to find the root cellar. Old houses like these usually had one. We could crawl out there. But after milling around in the dark, barking my shins, and coming dangerously close to dropping Woody on his head, I decided it was hopeless. The fire now showed through cracks in the floor, and the basement had begun to fill with smoke. We didn't have time to look any longer.

I came to a wall and felt my way along it until I came to a window. I couldn't see outside, only the window glaring back at me. It seemed as determined to keep me in here as I was determined to get out. I took it as a personal challenge.

Setting Woody against the wall, I reached up for the window. I could touch the bottom of it, but that was all. Still, there was a shelf about six inches wide that ran along the wall beneath the window. It offered a hand-hold of sorts, if I could find the strength to use it.

I reached up and gave it a try. I thought I could make it, but not with Woody draped over my shoulder. Maybe at the start of the night, but not now. I'd lost too much of me.

I searched the basement floor for something to swing and found a board that fit the bill. I closed my eyes and swung at the window. It exploded on contact, as the balmy night came pouring in and doused me with the sweetest air

I'd ever tasted. Then something heavy fell upstairs, jolting the floor and showering the basement with sparks. Not much time left. The floor was growing thinner by the minute. Once Nellie's bed came crashing through, it would pull the rest of the mansion down with it.

I pulled Woody to his feet and tried to lean him against the wall under the window. He wouldn't stay. As soon as I'd get him upright, he'd slide back down the wall again. More fire now showed through the cracks in the floor and began to drip at my feet. The night continued to pour in through the open window, roaring at me on its way to the fire. I could barely see outside. The window seemed to be shrinking, as the fire closed in on me. A few minutes more and I'd never make it out.

I shook Woody; then again. "Damn it! Do you want to live or not?" No answer. He might already be dead. No. He still had a strong pulse.

Then I remembered the board I'd used to break the window. I went down on my hands and knees looking for it, cut my hand on a piece of glass, and instinctively tried to suck away the blood. It tasted like copper and smoke and made me sick to my stomach.

I finally found the board, leaned it against the wall, and hung Woody by his shirt on it. He looked awkward hanging there, like I'd just crucified him. Something fell directly above me, and for an instant I thought it was the bed, as sparks flew everywhere, biting as they landed. Still Woody didn't move, even as the sparks swirled like gnats around his face.

I brushed the glass from the ledge, got a handhold and worked by way up until I could grasp the window frame. Pressing my palms flat against the outside of the frame, I wormed my way through the opening, avoiding the jagged glass along the edge of the frame. Once outside I used my feet to smash the remaining glass at the bottom of the window. Then I reached back inside for Woody.

So near, yet so far. I could reach the top of his head

and that was all. If I reached any further, I might topple back into the basement.

I grasped a handful of hair and tried to pull him closer. I felt the hair, greasy and unwashed, slide through my fingers, as Woody slipped a little lower on the board. I tried again with the same result. I broke into a cold sweat and fought the panic welling up inside me.

I was running out of time. Fire had eaten its way into the basement and now ran along the floor joists, fanned by the wind that rushed in through the window. The roar in my ears continued to grow. It seemed the fire was within me, eating away the last of my will. I felt small and weak, unable even to save myself, as inch by inch Woody continued to slip away from me, until I clung to a few brittle hairs that began to break one by one.

It was then I heard laughter. It began softly. Hesitant, tremulous, like butterfly wings opening for the first time, it wanted to soar, but couldn't. It lacked the heart. Instead, it tinkled cynically, like broken china swept from a dusty shelf, rising all the while, gaining momentum as it went, until it reached the high-pitched whinny of a horse laugh. Still clinging to Woody, I covered my ear with my free hand. Nellie's laughter grew louder. When the last strand of hair broke and Woody slipped out of reach, I covered both ears and ran. I tripped on a tree root and all went black.

I awakened with one hand clutching the fence that separated the yard from the corn field. I didn't know how I got there, whether I walked or crawled, but I'd been there long enough for my hand to go dead. As I worked my fingers, trying to get the blood flowing again, I could feel the heat from the fire on my face. I didn't want to look at it. Not now. Not ever. I didn't want to be reminded that I was mortal and mortals fail—and die. Something in me couldn't even take it seriously. My last words for Woody

220

were the refrain of an old song, "So long, it's been good to know you."

A firetruck pulled up and the firemen shot the first hissing geyser of water that exploded a window and sent flames racing for the roof. Already orange ribs showed through cracks in the mortar and the clouds overhead blossomed with a roseate glow. It was a fantastic sight, one of rage and power and perverse beauty, and it sent a chill through me that found the marrow of my bones.

More men and more cars and more firetrucks arrived. Though I was close enough to feel the heat and taste the smoke, I really wasn't part of this scene. I was Garth the Defeated and they were ants scurrying back and forth from the house, as the trucks whirred and ground, the hoses filled like fat snakes, and fountains of water burst like fireworks in the air. They cursed and ran and sprayed the fire at long range from all sides. When that didn't work, they attacked with axes and ladders, but it drove them back in an ever-widening circle. They called in more men and more trucks from nearby towns, but they couldn't stop it now, not if they'd had a hundred trucks.

Still they tried. They bombed at long range until they were walking in mud. They tightened the circle. They smiled at each other, their streaked and blackened faces relaxing for the first time. They gave each other hearty shouts of encouragement and moved in for the kill. Then they ran out of water, as one by one the geysers stopped and an orange tower of flames rose skyward.

Fire was everywhere now. Whipped by the wind, it spread to the corn field and the nearby trees. It trapped a group of firemen who had to run for their lives, leaving their truck behind. It dropped hot ash on my face and burned in patches on all sides of me. But I had nothing to fear. I'd been there when it started, right in the heart of hell. It hadn't got me then; it wouldn't get me now.

Finally it routed the spectators and drove them back to their cars, which clogged Fair Haven Road all the way back to Oakalla and kept the trucks from going for more water. Unchallenged, it ravaged the mansion, first gutting it, then cutting it down wall by wall until it sank under its own weight.

Two hours later I was alone at the fire site. No one had come to question me. I hadn't offered any answers. The abandoned firetruck still smoldered, its tires now black puddles, its once shiny red paint neither shiny nor red. The lane and the yard looked like a football game had been played in the rain. The apple trees had the bare dead look of winter, and I was sure I'd eaten my last Golden Pippin.

I took a last look at the ruins of the mansion. Woody was in there someplace. They might find him and they might not. I knew I didn't have the heart to look. I started back toward Oakalla just as the first drops of rain fell.

23

Rupert and I were on our way to Woodhollow Sanitarium. He'd met me along Fair Haven Road. He and Elvira had been to the show, their first in over a year. I told him that he picked a hell of a time to go. Then I filled him in on what had happened and what I knew.

"You can't blame yourself," he finally said.

"I don't know who else to blame."

"Look around. There's always somebody."

The gate to Woodhollow Sanitarium was unmanned and unlocked. We drove in unchallenged and parked where I had the day before. In the rain the sanitarium looked bloated and lifeless, overburdened with its thick eaves and massive walls and the weight of the past thirty years. Its segmented windows glared dully at us, like huge insect eyes that couldn't make up their minds whether to close in slumber or open a yawning mouth and swallow us whole.

I looked for the Cadillac. I didn't see it. I looked for Woody's red pickup. I didn't see it either. But the black Mercedes was there.

We walked to the front door of the sanitarium and rang the bell. No one answered. We rang it again and got the same result. I tried the door. It was unlocked. We decided to go on in.

We walked down the hall to Davids's office. A light was on inside. Rupert went in first, since he was the one with the gun. I limped in after him.

Davids didn't even bother to look at us. Instead, he sat slumped in a walnut captain's chair staring at the wall, like the deposed chairman of the board. I knew the feeling.

I glanced around his office. It came complete with landscapes, fireplace, a stuffed owl on a birch slab, and an ornate roll-top desk that ordinarily I would have admired. Not tonight though. There wasn't much about Dr. Abram Davids that I found admirable.

We sat in straight-back walnut chairs facing him. He had a bandage over his right eye, his nose was red and swollen, so was his finger where I'd bitten him, and his face was bruised in several places. He truly looked like a beaten man. I thought I knew why, and it had nothing to do with me.

Rupert read him his rights while Davids stared at the wall. His eyes were red and bleary, like he'd been crying. Then I noticed the photograph in his hand.

Nellie was wearing an ankle length blue wool suit, a tepid smile, and looked like she wished she were somewhere else. Davids was wearing a brown pin-striped suit, a brown broad-rimmed hat, and couldn't have been happier. The photograph had been taken some thirty-plus years ago on a cliff overlooking what appeared to be Lake Superior.

Davids noticed me staring at the photograph. "It was the fall of 1953," he said. "We were on our honeymoon."

"Long time ago," I said.

"Long time ago," he agreed.

Rupert nodded to make it a consensus.

"So why don't you tell us about it?" I said.

"About what?"

"You and Nellie."

"What's the point? By now you know what I am, what she is. What more is there to learn?"

"The truth."

He laughed at that. It was a dead laugh, without tone or humor. "Aren't you a little old to still believe there is such a thing, and that if there is, we are capable of understanding it?" Then he caught himself, let his arm fall in surrender. "It's no use. I have nothing to defend anymore. I'm not even allowed my cynicism. What is it you want to know?"

"You and Nellie. Why once she was in here and you saw what she was, you ever let her out in the first place."

"That's easy. I was seduced by Nellie's beauty. That and my own vanity. I was fresh out of the university and sure of my destiny. As we all are at that time in our lives, especially those of us who have never ventured beyond our cloistered ivy walls. I was no match for Nellie. I equated beauty with goodness. Surely there could be no evil within anyone as lovely as she. At least nothing consciously evil. Mischief perhaps, the mischief of a petulant child who wants nothing less than her own way, but not *evil*." He held onto the word, still perplexed by its power over him, as if holding it out for examination would somehow weaken it. "Dr. Prater, who was chief of staff, tried to warn me, but I wouldn't listen to him. I was as certain as he was cautious. And in the end my passion and my certainty convinced him that Nellie was no threat to her parents, that it was they who had precipitated the events that led to the violent act against her mother, that she was merely striking out blindly at what she perceived as injustice. And given her history as an orphan, when the very act of survival encouraged violence, it was the perfectly normal thing to do. So we released her. Dr. Prater signed the papers, informed her foster parents, and they came after her. It wasn't a day later that I discovered the missing barbiturates. It was a week after that we learned the Metzgers had been killed. I can't describe my thoughts. I felt I'd killed them as surely as if I'd given them the drugs myself."

"Did you ever confront Nellie? Ask her what really happened?"

"I didn't have to. She told me. She said it was easy. They were creatures of habit. They did everything the same way at the same time every day. So she drugged their oatmeal, knowing it would take effect on their way to church."

"Is that what she did to Big-Ears Brainard?"

"Yes. Only with him she used rat poison. She put it in his buttermilk."

"Thinking she'd get his money?"

"Yes. She'd seen him hide it in his bed, that monstrosity there on the second floor. He had a chamber hollowed out in it where he kept the money."

"What went wrong? Why didn't she get the money?"

"Nellie didn't know. One night it was there in the bed. The next night, when she went to look for it, it was gone."

"What night was that?"

"The night after she poisoned him."

"She poisoned him, not knowing where the money was?"

"No. She poisoned him, thinking the money was in the bed. He took a drive every Sunday after dinner. Alone. He never took Nellie along. She thought he would die on the road, as her parents had, and no one would be the wiser. But it didn't work out that way. He was tougher than she thought he was."

I thought of Big-Ears hiding the Cadillac in the straw,

226

even as his guts were burning up with poison, then walking away. And he might have made it back, too—if he hadn't fallen in the well. "When did Nellie realize the money was in the Cadillac?"

"Not until years later. Then she only guessed." He studied me. He saw how beaten-down I was. He must have thought he'd found an ally. "I know your next question. Knowing what she was, why did I ever marry her? I don't have an answer. Not even for myself. But Nellie was right today when she told you I married her for love. I did love her." He covered his face with his hand. "God help me, I still do."

I nodded. I understood. If you closed your eyes tightly enough and let your heart take over, there was much of Nellie to love—especially if you were vain enough to think you could change her.

"That's why you dug the holes at the Brainard Mansion? You were looking for Nellie's money, trying to raise yourself in her eyes?"

"Yes," he admitted. "I didn't give a damn about the money, but I knew Nellie did. She wanted it desperately. She said she'd earned every penny of it, and she'd walk through hell to have it." He looked up at me, wanting someone to understand. "I knew Nellie didn't love me. I knew she wasn't capable of loving anyone. But I thought that if I treated her with kindness and respect, that if I gave her the love and security she needed, she would at least be grateful and stay here with me. I succeeded in part. I guess I should be satisfied with that. She stayed with me for over thirty years, longer than I ever dared to hope."

"Until Woody came along?"

He straightened momentarily, as his voice came to life. "Woody! Such an innocuous name! May God damn him to hell if there is such a place! We were doing fine until he came along."

"Raising and selling marijuana?"

He was suddenly evasive. "I don't know what you're talking about."

"I'm talking about a dead pilot and a barn full of marijuana. If doing fine includes murder and drug dealing, then you've got a damned convenient set of principles."

"No comment" was his answer.

Rupert gave me a stern look. It said let's get what we can while we can. Don't rock the boat if you don't have to.

"Okay, forget the marijuana," I said. "What about Woody?"

"He'd found Brainard's money. He didn't say where. He told Nellie he was leaving Oakalla, that he'd send her share to her as soon as he was safely on his way."

"That wasn't enough for Nellie?"

"No. She wanted it all. She got word to me, and I passed it along to Martinez, our handyman. We never let Woody out of the gate."

"Did Woody know that you and Nellie were married?"

"We never told him. I doubt he was smart enough to figure it out."

"Did anybody here at Woodhollow ever know?"

"Of course. But it was sort of an in-house secret. We looked after our own here."

"Then after you kidnapped Woody, you and Martinez went after the money?"

"Yes, we went after the money. But just as we arrived at Woody's, so did someone else. We talked it over and decided to come back another day." He sighed deeply and sank lower in his chair. "It was a mistake. Nellie was furious with me. She called me a coward and worse. . . . You can guess how it made me feel. But I was determined that it would be I who would find the money, not she. So I took away her keys to the Mercedes and told her I'd go back in the morning. I forgot about Woody's pickup. She

228

took it while I was asleep and drove back over there that same night."

That was why Harry Thompson had seen a woman driving Woody's pickup early Tuesday morning. It was also why the wrecking bar was in Stony Creek. Nellie had used it to pry loose the seats in the Cadillac, then thrown it away when I surprised her at Woody's. That was on Tuesday. But Davids hadn't come looking for Nellie until Wednesday morning. Then again Wednesday night when he knocked me out. Where had he been on Tuesday? I asked him.

"Something came up," he said. He didn't want to discuss it. I didn't blame him. The pilot had been killed right about that time. I couldn't help thinking that the pilot's death might never have happened if Nellie hadn't run away, and if Davids hadn't been so intent on proving himself to her.

"And tonight?" I asked.

He glanced at me, then looked away. "There was nothing personal with you. I'd finally learned from Woody through Pentothal where the money was. Giving him Pentothal was the only way to communicate with the fool, to get him to stop talking gibberish. The trouble was now that we knew for certain it was still in the Cadillac somewhere we didn't know where the Cadillac was. We had a chance at it earlier, when that woman was here spying on Nellie, but she gave Martinez the slip. Then you came today looking for Nellie. We knew you were getting close to us. It would be just a matter of time. That's why I sent Martinez after you, but he panicked when you turned the tables and started following him."

"Why in Woody's pickup? Why send him in it?"

"It was handy. It ran well. Besides, if something went wrong, you couldn't trace it to us."

I was tempted to ask him if he'd used Woody's pickup to haul the marijuana from the barn, but I didn't. For an unwelcome visitor, he'd sure got a lot of mileage out of Woody. We both had. And all Woody had got were two weeks of torture and a fiery death. Somehow that didn't seem quite fair.

Davids continued, "I had to act fast. I went to Woody and threatened him. He started talking gibberish again, worse than before. I lost control and began to strike him. I guess I hit him too hard. He went out and never regained consciousness. But before he did, when he was lying dazed on the floor, I asked him one last time where the Cadillac was. 'Garth.' He babbled. 'Garth.' We put two and two together and came up with you."

"Then what happened?"

"I got a phone call, then a click at the other end. I didn't like the feel of it. I decided that right or wrong it was time to move. We put Woody in the back of the pickup and covered him with a blanket. My plan was to get you there, knock you out with the ether, then set fire to the place. The gas can would be in Woody's hand, and Woody's pickup would be outside. By the time someone figured it all out, Nellie and I would be long gone from here."

"Except Nellie had other plans."

He sat very still. He looked on the verge of breaking. The truth, whose existence he denied, was about to meet him face-to-face. "Yes. Nellie had other plans."

"Nellie set the fire?"

He'd started to tremble. His voice was a hoarse whisper. "Yes. Nellie set the fire. She tried to . . . She tried . . ." He began to sob. He couldn't go on.

"Do you know where she is now?"

He shook his head.

"What about Martinez?"

He hesitated before he shook his head again. He knew, but wouldn't tell me.

I started to get up. I almost didn't make it. I felt like I'd rusted to the chair. I limped to the door, down the hall, and outside. Knowing Nellie as I now did, I had the sad sick feeling that Martinez and Woody's pickup weren't very far away.

I'd have rather thought Martinez was on his way to Mexico—a smile on his worried face, some traveling money in his pocket. I'd have rather thought that Woody and the pilot weren't dead, Nellie wasn't a murderous psychopath, and Davids was a good old boy who'd been dealt a bad hand. I'd have rather thought evil was a toothless old wolf who sometimes bayed at the moon and kept us up at night, but otherwise did little to disturb the tranquillity of our lives. I *did* like to think the best of life. But sometimes reality got in the way.

As I hobbled across the grounds of Woodhollow toward the gate, I thought I heard a car start. It sounded like the Cadillac.

I came to the gate. It was closed and locked. I wasn't surprised. It was just like Nellie to be out here waiting for Davids. And here I was, a crippled duck, who'd walked right into her car sights. I wasn't Davids. But I doubted Nellie knew that—or would have cared if she had.

My eyes on the parking lot, I started back toward the sanitarium. I soon saw I wasn't going to make it. Its lights off, its motor purring, the Cadillac glided from the parking lot and started toward me.

I changed directions. At any moment Rupert and Davids might come walking out the door of the sanitarium into the path of the Cadillac. Instead, I hobbled across the grounds toward the far end of Woodhollow. Neither gaining, nor losing, on me the Cadillac followed.

I began to hobble faster, trying to keep a tree between us. I thought about circling the same tree ad infinitum until the Cadillac got dizzy and fell over. But though it had momentarily stopped raining, the grass was still wet. I didn't want to slip and end up with tread marks on my head.

One look told me I was fast running out of real estate. The wrought iron fence was just ahead, and there wasn't so much as a thistle to hide behind. I stopped, looked at the fence, then back at the Cadillac, and thought better of it. We ducks were never too good at climbing fences.

The lights came on and momentarily blinded me. I turned away and stumbled toward the fence. I had a plan. It wasn't a great plan, but about the best I could do under the circumstances.

It was the same plan I'd used once as a kid when chased by Randy Sharp, the schoolyard bully. I'd run at three-quarter speed, letting him gain on me all the while. Then, when he was too close to stop, I'd fallen and rolled into his legs. He went flying over me and ended up wearing a gravel smile. It was the last time he ever chased me.

I could feel the ground tremble as the Cadillac closed in on me. I only hoped Nellie's aim was true. Twenty yards to the fence, then ten, then five. I pitched forward, flattening out against the ground, as the Cadillac passed over me, so close its exhaust singed my hair. It tore through the fence, careened along the edge of the ravine beyond, then toppled over, rolling twice before bouncing on its wheels and landing upright at the bottom of the ravine.

I got up and eased my way down the ravine to it. Nellie sat in the driver's seat, her head resting against the door. She appeared to be sleeping, but something in the way her head rolled said she wasn't. I reached in through the open window and laid my hand against her throat. I felt blood, but no pulse.

Then I saw the lights from the Cadillac shining on something red. I had to wonder, especially since the road that led into Woodhollow was only a short distance away.

I followed the ravine toward the blotch of red, as a trickle of rain water splashed under my feet. The closer I came, the more certain I was that it was Woody's pickup. I wasn't disappointed.

Its weight bowing a beech sapling, the pickup faced nose down into the ravine. I could see its tracks in the leaves where it had run down the hill from the road. It looked like a straight shot—a good sledding run in winter—at least until you hit bottom.

I opened the door and looked in the cab of the pickup. It was empty. But Martinez was in the bed, partially covered by a thick wool blanket. He wouldn't get cold. Not now. Not ever. He was dead.

There was dried blood matted in his hair at the back of his head. The base of his skull had been caved in. I looked for Woody's lug wrench, but didn't find it. I guessed it was what Nellie had used to hit Martinez before she started the fire.

In my search for the lug wrench, I did find something that would please Rupert and likely put the last nail in Davids's coffin. It was a marijuana plant—a little soggy at the moment, but enough to tell me where the marijuana from the barn had gone. If it wasn't in the sanitarium, Davids could probably tell us where it was. And, to keep his neck from being stretched, he might just do that.

I walked back to the Cadillac. Nellie hadn't moved. Before closing her eyes, I took a long look at her face. It was a sharp face, the skin tightly drawn over the bones, and even in death a beautiful face—smooth, untroubled, untouched by hate. No answers here. No hint of the madness within. Neither anger nor remorse. Neither giving nor forgiving. Nothing to take home with me.

I ran my hand over the Cadillac. Except for a smashed top, a ruptured fuel line that was still dripping gasoline, and a crinkle or two on the hood, it had survived the crash remarkably well. With Edgar's help, in a few weeks it would look as good as new.

But it had never brought anyone much luck. Not Clinton Bass, not Doc Airhart, not Big-Ears Brainard, not

Woody, not Nellie, not me. And while I didn't believe in jinxes, I believed in track records. The Cadillac's track record was one of violence and deception and death. It had too many marks against it to ever wipe the slate clean.

I opened the door and dragged Nellie from the Cadillac, laying her a safe distance away. I felt in my shirt pocket and found a kitchen match, left over from the last time I burned the trash. Some people can strike them with their thumbnails. I had to use a rock.

24

It was a typical November day—grey and cold, a peep of sunshine, followed by a spit of snow, a day that matched my mood in every way. Every day for the past week they'd dug through the rubble of the Brainard mansion. They hadn't found Woody yet. Nor had they found any trace of Big-Ears Brainard's money.

Now Thelma Osterday was missing, along with her car, suitcase, and some of her clothes. All they'd found when they searched her house was a bag of walnuts with my name on it. Ruth and I were busy cracking them in front of a fire. It was the highlight of my week.

"How do your ribs feel?" I asked.

Ruth was none the worse for her Sunday night bowl. She'd even bowled her average. But then she wouldn't have complained even if her ribs had hurt. She wouldn't have given me the satisfaction.

"They only hurt when I breathe," she said.

"That's something anyway."

"Or when I'm cracking walnuts."

"You can quit anytime you want."

"Thanks. I never thought you'd ask." She leaned back in her chair and settled in.

"You never told me what Aunt Emma had on Wilmer," I said.

"I thought I did."

"You started to. Then the coffee water boiled over, then Liddy Bennett called, then . . ."

"That's okay. I get the message. It's not what's in the ground that Wilmer wants. It's what's growing there. Walnut trees. Maybe two hundred fifty thousand dollars worth of them."

"Doesn't Paul Black know that?"

"Sure. Nearly everybody knows that. But they all think they're on the old quarry property. That's why they're all licking their lips, waiting for the old man Sigfried to die, so they can buy the place. But they're not on the quarry property. They're on Paul Black's property."

"How did Aunt Emma find out?"

"She got to nosing around the surveyor's office and found out about the survey Wilmer had made ten years back. Then she had her own made. It seems the line fence is in the wrong place and has been for nearly fifty years. There's a whole hillside involved."

"Which is where the walnut trees are?"

"Which is where the walnut trees are."

"What's Aunt Emma doing about it?"

"Nothing. She doesn't trust Wilmer. But she doesn't trust Paul Black either. She figures as long as old man Sigfried's alive there's nothing to worry about."

"What if he dies?"

"Then she'll just sit back and watch the fur fly. But Emma's no spring chicken herself. She figures it's a toss-up between her and old man Sigfried, as to who'll die first. It

236

might be something she'll never have to worry about. So why bother."

"Good for her."

"That's what I said." She noticed the question on my face. "Was there something else?"

"I guess not. But for some reason I thought Wilmer had something else up his sleeve, something to do with the Cadillac itself. In fact, he called me a couple days ago asking about it. I didn't have the heart to tell him I'd burned it. I just told him I didn't know where it was."

Ruth suddenly started cracking walnuts again. "You don't want to know."

"Sure I do. I'm a big boy now."

She cracked a walnut so hard that bits of shell went all over the floor. "Okay. But remember you asked for it. I called the Cadillac Motor Car division at General Motors. Guess how many Cadillac convertible sedans they made in 1936?"

I covered my ears. "Don't tell me."

"Six."

"I said not to tell me." I looked out the window at the sky. It was spitting snow again. Appropriate. "Did they give you a dollar value?"

"It was, in their words, priceless."

"If you buy the rope, I'll make the noose."

"For which one of us? I had it in my hands, remember? And wouldn't take it." She sorted through some letters on the end table beside her chair. "Here, this might cheer you up. It came for you yesterday."

"What's that?"

She sailed an envelope at me. "This."

I let it lie on the floor a moment. "Is it from Diana?"

"I don't know. I didn't open it."

"First time for everything." I picked up the envelope and opened it. There was a card inside with a possum on the front. I turned the card over. Along with a smiling face that Thelma had drawn was the message: California here we come! It was signed, Thelma and *Woody*! "I'll be damned!" I said.

"What's that?" I got up and handed the card to Ruth. After she read it, she said. "That makes two of us."

I walked to the phone and called Rupert at the number Elvira had given me. He answered on the tenth ring. "This better be important," he said. "We've got a bonfire here as high as the trees. You can guess what we're burning. And if the wind shifts, half the county might end up walking on air." After a week of searching, Rupert was finally satisfied he'd found all the marijuana.

"You'll never guess whom I got a card from."

"No, I probably won't."

"Try."

"Garth, I don't have time. A cow's been nosing around here all day. Now she just wandered over into the line of fire. The next thing I know, she'll be trying to jump over the moon."

"Thelma Osterday."

"Thelma? Where in the world is she?"

"I don't know. I can't read the postmark."

"What did she have to say? Wait a minute, Garth. The cow just took the plunge. Right now she's trying to climb a telephone pole. I've got to chase her out of there before she does."

"I haven't got to the best part."

"Well, hurry. That cow's got a dead bead on oblivion."

"Thelma wasn't the only one who signed it. Woody Padgett did too."

There was a long silence on his end. "It's not possible, is it?"

"I didn't think so. But somehow I got to the fence. I thought I crawled. Maybe somebody carried me."

"Woody?"

"Who else? Wilmer calls him Possum, says he's the best at it he ever saw."

"I'll be damned," he muttered. Then he shouted, "Got to go, Garth! Bossie's already to the first rung!"

I hung up the phone. I looked out the window at the flurry of snow. Behind me the fire crackled contentedly. I searched through my wallet, found Diana's number, and called her. It just seemed the thing to do.

Today her line wasn't busy. Better yet, she was home.